Fairy Realm

Enter the Realm

Fairy Realm

Enter the Realm

EMILY RODDA

ILLUSTRATIONS BY RAOUL VITALE

HARPERCOLLINS*PUBLISHERS*

Library of Congress Cataloging-in-Publication Data
Rodda, Emily.
    Enter the Realm : three adventures / Emily Rodda ; illustrations by
Raoul Vitale. — 1st ed.
        v.   cm. — (Fairy realm ; [bk. 1–3])
    "The Charm Bracelet, The Flower Fairies, and The Third Wish were
originally published under the name Mary-Anne Dickinson as the
Storytelling Charms Series, 1994"—T.p. verso.
    Summary: Presents the first three books in the Fairy Realm series in
which Jessie discovers the magical Realm and has many adventures.
    Contents: The charm bracelet — The flower fairies — The third wish.
    ISBN-10: 0-06-120845-0 (trade bdg.)
    ISBN-13: 978-0-06-120845-4 (trade bdg.)
    [1. Fairies—Fiction. 2. Magic—Fiction. 3. Wishes—Fiction.]
I. Vitale, Raoul, ill. II. Title.
PZ7.R5996Ent 2007   2006103264
[Fic]—dc22   CIP
                                                                AC

Typography by Karin Paprocki
2 3 4 5 6 7 8 9 10

First Edition

CONTENTS

Fairy Realm

BOOK 1

The Charm Bracelet

CONTENTS

CHAPTER ONE

The secret garden

J essie felt better once she was in the secret garden. She sat down right in the center of its smooth, small square of lawn and looked around.

Yes, here at least nothing at all had changed. This place still made her feel as safe and peaceful as it always had. Clustered around the edges of the lawn, her grandmother's favorite spiky gray rosemary bushes still filled the air with their sweet, tangy smell. Behind them the tall, clipped hedge still rose high on every side. When Jessie was little, she used to think the hedge made this part of her grandmother's garden very special. Its wall of leaves seemed to keep the whole world out.

But, thought Jessie, clasping her hands around her knees, it doesn't keep the world out. Not really. The secret garden's just a place at the bottom of Granny's real garden. It's a place where I can be alone for a while, and pretend things are still the way they were before Granny fell and sprained her wrist. Before Mum started worrying about Granny living alone, and decided she *must*, absolutely must, move out of Blue Moon, her big old house in the mountains, and come to live with us.

She remembered the last time she and her mother, Rosemary, had come to stay with Granny. It had been winter, nearly three months ago. There had been no talk of Granny moving then. Then, things had been very different.

Jessie had always loved winter at Blue Moon. Every evening, as it got dark, they would light a fire in the living room, and then Jessie and her mother would sit cuddled up on the big squashy chairs watching the flames while Granny made dinner.

"No, I don't want help. You sit down and rest,

6

Rosemary," Granny would say to Mum. "You work too hard. Let me look after you—just while you're here. I love to do it." And after a few minutes' protest, Mum would agree, and settle back gratefully, smiling.

Then for a while the only sounds they would hear would be the popping and snapping of the fire, the purring of Granny's big ginger cat, Flynn, crouched on a rug, and Granny's voice as she moved around the kitchen, singing the sweet songs that Jessie remembered from when she was a baby. There was one song that she had always especially loved. *Blue Moon floating, mermaids singing, elves and pixies, tiny horses* . . . it began. Jessie thought Granny had probably made it up, because it didn't rhyme, and the tune was lilting and strange.

Inside Blue Moon it was warm, cozy and safe. Outside, huge trees stretched bare branches to a cold black sky that blazed with stars, and in the morning a dusting of white frost crackled under your feet when you walked on the grass.

It had always seemed strange and magical to

Jessie. At home there were no big trees and no frost. And the city lights seemed to drown the brightness of the stars.

But if winter in the mountains was magical, spring was even better. In spring everything sparkled. The bare trees began to bud with new leaves of palest green, and in their shade bluebells and snowdrops clustered. Bees buzzed around the lilac bushes that bent their sweet, heavy heads beside the house. Butterflies of every color and size danced among the apple blossom. In spring it was as if Blue Moon was waking up after a long sleep. Everywhere there were new beginnings.

But not this spring, Jessie thought sadly. This spring was more like an ending. She'd been feeling sad ever since her mother had told her about the plan to take Granny home with them at the end of this visit.

"Don't you want Granny to live with us, Jessie?" her mother had finally asked her, as they drove up the winding road that led from the city to the mountains. "You two have always been so close, especially since your dad died. I thought you'd love the idea."

Jessie tried to explain. "It's just that . . . I can't really imagine Granny away from Blue Moon," she said. She turned her head away, pretending to look out the window, but really not wanting her mother to see the tears she could feel prickling in her eyes. "And . . . I'll miss . . . coming up here," she burst out. "I'll miss the house, and the trees, and the secret garden."

"Oh, darling, of course you will!" Mum took one hand off the steering wheel to stroke Jessie's long red hair. "So will I. Blue Moon's my old home, remember. I love it, just like you do. But Jessie, it's been five years since Grandpa died. And you know how worried I've been about Granny living all alone without anyone to look after her." She smiled. "My dad might have been the artist in the family, but he was a very practical man all the same. You wouldn't remember, I suppose. But he was sensible, and took no risks. Which is more than you can say for Granny, bless her heart."

Jessie in fact did remember Grandpa quite well, even though she'd been so young when he died. His name was Robert Belairs. His paintings had been sold all over the world and were in many books. But to Jessie he was just Grandpa, a tall, gentle man with kind blue-gray eyes, a short white beard and a beautiful smile. She remembered how he always let her watch him paint in his upstairs studio at Blue Moon. And she remembered the paintings he worked on there—the soft, misty mountain landscapes, and the fairyland scenes for which he'd become so famous.

It was the fairy pictures that Jessie had especially loved. Sitting quietly on a stool beside him, she used to watch with wonder as a fantasy world came to life under her grandfather's brush, a mysterious and beautiful world full of golden light. Lots of these paintings hung on the walls of Blue Moon, because every year, on Granny's birthday, Grandpa had painted a special picture just for her. He'd finished the last one just before he died.

Robert Belairs' fairyland was a world of pretty cottages, treehouses and shining castles, and elfin-faced people in wonderful floating clothes. He always called these people "the Folk." The most beautiful and royal-looking of the women had long golden-red hair and green eyes like Jessie's own. This had pleased her very much, though she knew that Grandpa wasn't really painting her. He'd always painted his fairy princesses that way. People used to laugh and say that was why he'd fallen in love with her grandmother in the first place. Granny's hair was white now, of course, but when she had first come to Blue Moon to marry Robert Belairs her hair had been as red as Jessie's.

Grandpa's paintings were also full of busy gnomes, dwarfs, pixies and elves, thin little brownies, and tiny flower and rainbow fairies with gossamer wings. There were sometimes miniature horses, too, their manes threaded with ribbons and tiny bells. Jessie had really loved those. She had thought her grandfather was very clever to be able to paint such pictures. Maybe he was a bit magical himself.

And yes, she remembered how carefully he had looked after Granny, too. When Mum and Jessie had visited Blue Moon in those days, it was Granny who cooked the delicious food they ate, who talked

11

and laughed, who suggested all sorts of outings and adventures and never expected anything to go wrong. But it was Grandpa who packed the extra box of matches for the picnic, "just in case." It was Grandpa who took the umbrella when they went on a walk, "just in case." It was Grandpa who made sure there were spare keys to all the doors, "just in case."

Granny used to tease him about it. She'd reach up to pat his cheek, the gold charm bracelet she always wore jingling on her wrist. "You always expect the worst, Robert. Don't worry so. All will be well," she'd say. And he'd smile, and touch her hand. "Better to be safe than sorry, princess," he'd answer. And quite often he was right.

Jessie could understand why Mum thought Granny couldn't exist safely without him. But she just knew Mum was wrong. Her mind went back to the argument they'd had in the car on the way up to Blue Moon.

"Granny tripped over that stray kitten that came in!" she'd protested. "That had nothing to do with being alone, Mum. That could happen to any-

12

one, any time. And she only sprained her wrist."

"But Jessie, it could have been so much worse!" Her mother had frowned. "If she'd hurt her leg or something she could have lain there in pain for days without being able to call for help." Her hands had tightened on the steering wheel. "You have to be sensible about this, Jessie," she'd said firmly. "And so does Granny. Both of you have to listen to me for a change. What's needed round here is a bit of common sense!"

Now, sitting in the secret garden, Jessie realized that her mother was really very like Grandpa. She had his kind blue-gray eyes and his strong practical streak. She wasn't like Granny at all. But Jessie was. She knew that quite well. For one thing, she looked like Granny. She was going to be taller, of course: that was obvious, since already they were about the same height. Jessie wore an old gray cloak of Granny's for a dressing gown when she came to stay at Blue Moon, and even when she was in bare feet it didn't trail on the ground.

It was from Granny that Jessie had inherited her red hair, green eyes and pointed chin. She had been named Jessica after Granny, too. But, more important than name or looks, Jessie and her grandmother shared a love of stories, songs and fantasy that made them really enjoy each other's company.

And there was something else. They simply understood each other. Jessie always knew how Granny was feeling about things, and Granny always knew how Jessie was feeling, too. It had been like that ever since Jessie could remember.

Was that why, when Jessie had run into Granny's bedroom after they'd arrived at Blue Moon an hour ago, she had immediately felt so worried and sad? Was that why she hadn't been able to bear staying there, but had had to escape to the secret garden? Was that why . . . ?

Jessie sat perfectly still. Without warning, a thought had whirled into her mind. She began to shiver, her eyes wide and startled, her hands gripping the soft grass. Suddenly she had become terribly sure of something. Granny was in trouble. Real trouble. It wasn't just a matter of a sprained wrist, or sadness, or loneliness. It was something far more dangerous.

She sprang to her feet. She didn't know where the thought had come from. But now it was there, she knew it was true. And she had to do something about it. She didn't know what. But she had to help. She had to!

She began running for the house.

CHAPTER TWO

The Missing Bracelet

At her grandmother's bedroom door Jessie hesitated. Her heart was thumping. She smoothed her tangled hair and tried to calm down. Mum and Nurse Allie would still be with Granny. They'd be alarmed if she burst into the room in a panic.

She felt the soft tap of a paw on her ankle, gasped with fright, and looked down to meet the solemn golden eyes of Flynn, her grandmother's cat. He had been sitting so quietly in the dim hallway that she hadn't noticed him. She crouched to stroke his soft fur.

"Are you keeping guard on Granny's door, Flynn?" she asked him. "Won't Nurse Allie let you inside?"

He stared at her, unblinking.

"She would, you know, if only you wouldn't fight with the gray kitten," Jessie whispered, moving her hand around to scratch him under the chin. "It wasn't the kitten's fault that Granny fell, you know, Flynn. It was an accident."

Flynn rumbled in his throat, a noise more like a growl than a purr.

"Don't worry," Jessie soothed him. "Granny will be feeling better soon. Nurse Allie's going home now that we're here. Mum's a nurse, too, and Granny will be quite all right with her. So tonight I'll let you into Granny's room. The kitten can stay out, for a change. Everything's going to be all right, Flynn."

But when she opened the door and slipped into the bedroom, she wasn't so sure. When they'd first arrived, Granny had been sitting in her comfortable chair by the window. Now she was lying in bed, looking pale and ill. Rosemary was sitting beside her, hands clasped on the flowery bedcover, while in the corner of the room Nurse Allie, plump and busy, measured out medicine. The little gray kitten, Flynn's enemy, purred softly on the window seat.

Granny's long white hair, braided into a thick plait, trailed over the pillows. One wrist was heavily bandaged. The bandage was much more obvious now that she was lying down and her arm was out of the sling she'd been wearing earlier.

She smiled faintly at Jessie. "Where have you been, Jessie?" she asked. Even her voice sounded different. It seemed to have lost its music.

"I've been to the secret garden," Jessie said, moving over to stand beside the bed.

Granny smiled again. "Oh, yes," she murmured. "The secret garden. You love it, don't you, Jessie?"

"Maybe you could come there with me, tomorrow morning," Jessie suggested eagerly, taking her hand.

"Well, that might be a little difficult for Granny, dear," beamed Nurse Allie, bringing the medicine

19

over to the bed. "But you could sit out on the front verandah for a while, Mrs. Belairs, couldn't you? The fresh air would do you the world of good. Cheer you up!"

"We'll see," said Granny softly. "I just feel . . . so tired." Her eyelids fluttered closed.

Jessie looked despairingly around the room. Why was Granny like this? She saw that Nurse Allie was shaking her head at Mum in disappointment. Cheerful Nurse Allie, with her crisp curls and smart uniform, had tried very hard to make things pleasant for Granny while she waited for Mum and Jessie to come.

She'd used every trick she knew to brighten up the bedroom. She'd brought in vases of spring flowers. She'd opened the curtains to let in the sunshine. She'd let the gray kitten play on the rug. She'd noticed that the dark, mysterious painting on the wall facing the bed, the last painting Grandpa had done before he died, made Granny cry, so she'd taken it away and put a pretty mountain scene in its place.

But nothing had worked. Granny lay quiet and

listless in her bed, or sat obediently in her chair, without showing any sign of cheering up or getting well.

Jessie was still for a moment. Then she noticed something. She stared. Why hadn't she noticed this before?

"Granny, where's your bracelet?" she asked. Never before had she seen Granny without her gold bracelet, so thickly hung with charms that it tinkled on her wrist with every movement.

The old woman's eyelids slowly opened. "Bracelet?" she mumbled. She looked confused, and then there was a flash of memory and panic in her eyes. Her fingers tightened on Jessie's hand. "It's lost!" she muttered. "Jessie . . . it's gone. They . . . must have taken it off while they were fixing my wrist." She struggled to rise from her pillow. "Jessie, you must find it for me. You must! I need it!"

"Now, now, don't let's get ourselves into a froth!" crooned Nurse Allie, frowning at Jessie. She pressed Granny gently back on to the pillows. "Now, we've been through all this, dear. We know the bracelet must be somewhere, don't we? It's quite safe. It's been put away in some drawer or other, that's all."

"I must have it!" protested Granny, moving her head restlessly.

"You just concentrate on getting better, Mum," said Rosemary. "We'll worry about the bracelet later."

"But time is running out! It's nearly my seventieth birthday!" Granny cried. Then she stopped, and a strange, puzzled expression crossed her face. "My birthday? Why does that matter?" she whispered.

Nurse Allie stepped forward briskly. "A little rest is what you need, I think, dear," she said, shooting a warning look at Rosemary and Jessie. "All this excitement! Goodness me!"

"Sorry, Nurse," said Rosemary. She stood up and pushed Jessie a little crossly to the door. Jessie could see there was no point in arguing. Both Mum and Nurse Allie thought she was making Granny upset. She let herself be ushered from the room.

Flynn looked at Jessie and her mother with

wide eyes as they closed the door softly behind them, but he made no move to follow them out to the back of the house. He just settled back to his guard duty, still as a statue, in the dim hallway.

"Jessie, you mustn't worry Granny," Rosemary said sternly as they reached the kitchen. "Not about the charm bracelet, or the secret garden, or anything. She's not well. She has to have peace and quiet." She began pulling things out of cupboards, getting ready to start dinner. Then she turned around and tried to smile.

"Look, darling, don't worry too much," she said. "It's only natural for Granny to be depressed. Just think about it. Her wrist must be very sore. And it's her birthday the day after tomorrow. It wasn't long after her birthday five years ago that Grandpa died. It makes her sad to think about it."

"But Mum . . ." Jessie looked at her mother's kind, worried face and thought better of what she'd been about to say. Mum wouldn't understand about the feeling of danger she'd had in the secret garden. And she wouldn't understand why she felt the charm bracelet was so important. After all, Jessie didn't really understand it herself!

All Jessie knew was that Granny was in trouble. And that the charm bracelet she always wore was missing. And that for some reason the bracelet had to be found before Granny's birthday the day after tomorrow. Jessie clenched her fists. She made herself a promise that she would find the bracelet if she had to look behind every cushion and in every drawer in the house to do it! After dinner she'd check Granny's room. Then she'd do the living room and the kitchen. She'd be sure to find it before bedtime.

But bedtime came and still the bracelet had not been found.

Jessie lay cuddled up in bed in the small room that was always hers at Blue Moon and thought hard. Of course there were many more places she could look. But she couldn't see how the bracelet could have got into one of the spare rooms, for example, or the dining room, or the sunroom either.

She closed her eyes. The bed was warm and

soft, and the sheets smelled faintly of rosemary. She was very tired. Her thoughts began to drift. In the morning she'd try again. In the morning . . .

Her eyes flew open again. She could have sworn she'd heard a very faint tinkling sound. It sounded just like the charm bracelet when it jingled on Granny's wrist. And it had come from outside, in the garden. She was sure of it.

She threw back the covers, jumped out of bed and ran to the window. Outside, grass and flowers shone in the moonlight. The trees held their budding branches up to the sky, throwing deep shadows on the lawn. Jessie strained her eyes, but there was nothing more to be seen. Nothing but the gray kitten, slinking through the trees toward the secret garden.

Jessie shivered. She left the window and ran back to bed, jumping in and pulling the covers tightly around her. There was no one out there. She must have imagined the sound. She closed her eyes again and tried not to think about the bracelet. Again the warmth of the bed stole around her. Then, suddenly, she thought of a place she hadn't looked. When Nurse Allie had taken Grandpa's painting off Granny's bedroom wall, she'd put it in his studio for safekeeping. Jessie heard her tell Mum so. Maybe she'd absent-mindedly put the bracelet there, too.

The more Jessie thought about it, the more likely it seemed. The studio. First thing in the morning, she'd look there. With a sigh of relief she turned on her side, and in a few moments was asleep.

CHAPTER THREE

The Call

The next morning, before breakfast, Jessie went to Grandpa's studio. She turned the key in the door and let herself in. It was a big, beautiful room painted white. The early morning light streamed through its tall windows.

Jessie sighed. The room reminded her so much of Grandpa. It still smelled of paint, canvas and paper. The stool she had always sat on while she was watching him paint stood in one corner. His paints and brushes, sketchpads and other things lay on the bench as though he was about to come and use them any minute.

She noticed that the picture Nurse Allie had taken from Granny's room was leaning against a table near the door. She looked at it curiously. It certainly wasn't as pretty as most of the others Grandpa had done, she decided. It was dim and very mysterious looking, and there were no people, animals or fairies in it. It showed an archway in a wild-looking dark green hedge covered with splodges of gray. Through the archway you could dimly see what lay beyond—a pebbly road, a few shadowy bushes and a gray sky in which a pale blue moon floated. A blue moon, thought Jessie. Grandpa must have been thinking about this house when he painted that.

Carefully she tipped the painting forward so she could look at the back. She knew Grandpa often put the names of his paintings there. But this time there was no name. Only a white card, painted with a sprig of rosemary, and some words in Grandpa's firm, looping handwriting: *For my princess on her birthday. Better to be safe than sorry. All my love, always, Robert.* Then there was a date. Almost exactly five years ago.

Holding her breath, Jessie gently let the painting tip back into place again. No wonder it made Granny cry. It mightn't be the prettiest picture Grandpa had painted, but it was his last present to her, and the message showed how much he'd loved her.

Biting her lip, Jessie looked around at the benches and shelves that lined the studio. Everything was neat and clean. Everything was in its place. There was no sign at all of the charm bracelet.

She left the studio and hurried to Granny's room. She found her sitting in her chair by the window, her arm in a white sling. Flynn, purring like rumbling thunder, was lying beside her. The gray kitten was nowhere to be seen. Granny looked up and smiled as Jessie came in and gave her a kiss.

"Your mother was wondering where you were, Jessie," she said. "I think she wants you to have breakfast."

"I've been looking for your bracelet, Granny," said Jessie eagerly. "I haven't found it yet, but I just came to tell you that you mustn't worry. I won't give up. I'm going to look everywhere till it's found."

Her grandmother's smile slowly faded and a puzzled line deepened between her eyebrows. "Bracelet?" she asked softly. "What bracelet is that, Jessie?"

Shocked, Jessie stared at her. "Your charm bracelet!" she burst out. "You know. The bracelet you always wear. The one that got lost."

"Oh . . ." Granny looked confused and uncertain. She raised her unbandaged hand to her forehead. Her fingers trembled slightly. "Oh . . . I'm sorry, dear. I'm . . . getting a bit forgetful, I think. I'm not quite sure . . ."

Flynn growled in his throat.

"Breakfast, Mum!" announced Rosemary's cheery voice. She came in bearing a tray of fruit, toast and tea, and put it down on a side table. "Oh, here you are, Jessie!" she exclaimed. "I didn't know where you'd got to."

Jessie looked from Granny to her mother and back again. Her throat felt tight. Only yesterday

Granny had been worrying herself sick about the charm bracelet. How could she have forgotten it so soon? She mumbled something, backed out the door and ran for the kitchen.

Jessie searched for the charm bracelet all day, but when night fell she still hadn't found it. And she was the only one who cared. Granny now seemed truly to have forgotten that the bracelet had ever existed. And Mum, busy packing and organizing things for the move back to town, was too distracted to think much about it.

"Don't worry yourself too much, Jessie," she said kindly that evening, as she watched Jessie going through the drawers in the living room yet again. "The bracelet's slipped down behind something, probably. Or got mixed up with some other stuff in Granny's room. It'll turn up in the end."

Maybe, thought Jessie. But not soon enough. Tomorrow's Granny's birthday. We're running out of time. She paused, confused by her own thoughts. Running out of time? For what? She closed the drawer in which she'd been searching, and rubbed her forehead with a tired hand. Mum had said not to worry but Jessie couldn't help it. And something else was worrying her far more than the missing bracelet.

She glanced at her mother. She couldn't keep it to herself any longer.

"Granny doesn't remember her bracelet any more!" she whispered. "When I talk to her about it she doesn't know what I mean!" She bent her head, tears in her eyes.

Rosemary's face softened. "Oh, Jessie, darling, don't be sad." She put her arm around Jessie's waist. "You know that sometimes when people get older they can be forgetful. And Granny hasn't been well. She had a bad shock when she fell. It's quite natural that she's a bit confused now. It's not something to be scared of or anything."

Jessie nodded and sniffed. "I know that," she said. "But Granny's not very old. She's only sixty-nine. Simone at school's great-grandmother is a hundred and one, and *she* remembers things. And anyway, Mum, whatever else Granny forgot, how could she forget the charm bracelet? She used to tell me every charm on it was a memory of something special. Every charm had a story. The heart, and the fish, and the apple, and the key, and . . ."

Her mother patted her shoulder. "I know," she soothed. "I know. It's hard for you to understand. But Granny's been living alone here for too long, Jessie. She's been living in the past. She'll be so much better when she's away from here. Believe me."

Jessie wasn't so sure. When she crawled into bed that night, her thoughts were racing around in her head so much that she was afraid she would lie awake all night. But she was very tired and it wasn't long before she was lulled to sleep in the warm, cozy bed.

She slept very deeply. The moon climbed higher in the sky and shone through the window, but Jessie slept on. There were sounds in the night but she didn't hear them. The hours slipped by. And then . . .

Thud! A heavy weight landed on Jessie's feet. She opened her eyes, blinking in the darkness.

Her heart pounded. What was happening? She felt something moving on the bedclothes. And then she was staring into the golden gaze of Flynn, and his soft paw was patting her cheek.

She wet her dry lips and sat up. "What is it?" she whispered. Flynn stared at her, then looked toward the window.

Jessie rubbed her eyes. Was this a dream? No, Flynn was really there, and again he was looking at the window. He jumped from the bed and walked over to it, his tail high. He looked back at her. He wanted her to come with him.

Jessie got out of bed and went to the window just as she had the night before. She looked out. But again there was nothing to be seen. Not even the gray kitten, slinking among the trees. There was nothing . . .

And then she heard it. The faintest possible sound. A voice. She strained her ears to hear.

"Jessica! Jessica!"

Jessie's mouth fell open in shock. Someone was calling her name! She looked wildly at Flynn. He padded to the bedroom door, looking back at her over his shoulder.

"Flynn, what is it?" hissed Jessie. He went out the door and then came back in again. His golden eyes were fixed on hers. It was obvious that he wanted her to follow.

"Jessica!" The voice was a little clearer now. It sounded urgent, and tired, as though it had been calling for a long time.

Jessie ran to the corner cupboard and pulled out Granny's old gray cloak. It would be chilly in the garden. She threw the cloak around her shoulders and followed Flynn.

He padded to the back door and then stood back while she opened it and slipped outside into the cool night air.

"Aren't you coming with me?" she whispered, looking back at him. But somehow she knew the answer even before he sat down on the doorstep, head up, paws pressed together. He had to wait here. He had to guard Granny. That was his job. Jessie had to go into the night and answer the strange call alone.

She began to creep through the shadows on the

lawn. The voice was clearer now, though it was still faint. And she thought that behind it she could hear other voices.

"Jessica! Jessica! Oh, if you can hear me, hurry! Please hurry."

Jessie moved faster, holding the cloak tightly around her. She knew now where the call was coming from.

It was coming from the secret garden.

CHAPTER FOUR

"where am i?"

Holding her breath, Jessie pushed open the door in the hedge and stepped inside.

There was no one there. The scent of rosemary wafted about her as she stood motionless on the smooth grass. She took another step . . .

Suddenly there was a sighing, whispering sound, a rush of air against her face, and a swirl of mist clouding her eyes. Jessie's cloak snapped away from her fingers. Her hair blew, crackling, around her head. She gasped with fear.

And then she was no longer in the secret garden. She was no longer anywhere at all she

41

knew. And the voice was calling out in glee: "We've got her! I told you so! I told you . . ." and then it broke off and cried out in surprise and horror. "Oh, no! Oh no-o-o!"

Jessie gazed around her. She felt rather than saw that her cloak had slipped to the ground. Her hair was tangled on her shoulders. Far away she could hear singing.

She was standing on a pebbly road that ran beside a thick, dark hedge—a hedge much, much higher and stronger than the hedge of the secret garden, but marked all over with great gray patches of dead and dying wood. The air was sweet and shadowy. A memory stirred in her. Abruptly she looked up. There, sure enough, was a soft gray sky and, floating in it, a blue moon. But when she looked back at the hedge she could see no archway. There was no way she could tell how she had come through the hedge at all.

"This is a disaster!" snapped an angry voice.

Jessie spun around. Behind her, gaping at her in astonishment, were a fat little woman with eyes like black beads, her head wound up in a scarf; a thin, depressed-looking elf with long pointed ears that drooped at the tips; and a perfect miniature white horse with ribbons in its mane and a very cross expression on its face. Jessie was astounded to realize that it was the horse who had spoken.

"A disaster!" it growled again. "How could this have happened?" It rounded on the fat little woman. "Patrice! I thought you said . . ."

"This is definitely the Door," the woman called Patrice fluttered. "Maybelle, I promise you, it is *definitely*—"

"We're doomed!" wailed the elf. "Doomed! Now we've used up all the magic. And the Door's shut again! And we still haven't found her. We got some human child instead. Oh, doom! Doom! Oh I *knew* this would never work. I knew it!"

Jessie covered her mouth with both hands to stop herself from screaming. Where was she? Who were these people?

There was a shout and a stomping sound in the distance.

"Look out!" hissed Maybelle, shaking her mane. "The Royal Guard!"

"Oh, no!" squeaked the elf. He flapped his hands and began to run helplessly this way and that. "Oh, what next? Now we're for it! Now we're for it!"

"Hide her, Patrice! Quick! Over there!" ordered Maybelle, ignoring him.

Patrice put her arm around Jessie and hustled her away behind some nearby bushes. The noise of marching feet grew louder. With a last despairing squeak the elf leaped into the air and hung there, with his hands over his eyes.

Maybelle rolled her own eyes in disgust, then lowered her nose and began calmly to eat grass as if nothing at all unusual was happening.

"Stay still as still, dearie," breathed Patrice in Jessie's ear.

Jessie had no intention of moving. She had never been so scared in her life. She huddled close to the ground, hardly daring to breathe.

In a few moments a group of soldiers in smart uniforms marched out of the dimness. Their booted feet scrunched on the pebbles of the roadway. Patrice squeezed Jessie's hand in her own small one. Jessie trembled and she closed her eyes. Her cloak was still lying where it had fallen on the road. The soldiers were certain to see it there as they walked past. Then they would know a stranger was here. And they would start to search. And then . . .

"Halt!" The leading guard barked the order, and with a stamp the whole troop stopped dead, right in front of the spot where Jessie and Patrice were hiding.

"Five minutes' rest," said the leading guard. The word was passed along the line, and one by one the guards thankfully broke away from the line and sat down on the grass. The leader glanced at the shivering elf in the air and snorted with tired amusement. She stretched her back and looked at the moon. "It's midnight, Loris," she said to the man next to her. "The big day's come at last."

"They're cutting it a bit fine if you ask me," he answered gruffly. He flicked a finger at a bare patch in the dark, looming hedge. "This won't last much longer. They say sunrise marks the fifty years exactly. The Lady came back last night, didn't she? Why hasn't she fixed up the magic by now? Why wait till the last minute?"

The leader shrugged. "I suppose she knows what she's doing," she replied. "But I tell you what, I'll be glad to see the hedge back to normal again, Loris. It's dying fast. And without it we'll never keep the Others out. Too many of them."

The man grunted his agreement. "They say there are thousands of them, just waiting. They know the story. They've been hoping that the Lady won't come back. They've been hoping that the magic'll all run out, and the hedge'll die." He jerked his head to where Maybelle was innocently grazing nearby. "And you know what they'll do then," he added grimly.

Maybelle raised her head and shook her white mane.

Behind the bushes, Jessie felt Patrice's hand tighten on her own.

"Sshh!" warned the leader. "No point in getting creatures all upset. And anyhow, there's nothing to worry about, Loris. The Lady did come back, didn't she? Just like she said she would. And

46

today's the day. Listen to those mermaids singing. They've gathered in the Bay. Hundreds of them. They know it's time. By morning the hedge'll be its old self again."

"Lucky this magic business only happens once in a blue moon," growled Loris. "I don't like it."

"Can't say I care for it much either," grinned the leader. She pulled her cap straighter on her head. "All right, Loris. They've had enough of a rest. Let's get going."

Loris turned and shouted. Grumbling, the rest of the guards got up and formed into a line again.

"Forward!" barked the leader. And off the troop marched. Left, right, left, right, along the pebbled road. In a few moments everything was quiet again.

Carefully Patrice and Jessie clambered to their feet and crept out into the open. Jessie ran and picked up her cloak, which was still lying beside the hedge. It was a wonder that the guards hadn't noticed it, she thought. She hugged it to her for a moment. It was soft and warm, and smelled of home.

Maybelle trotted over to them. She glanced disdainfully up at the elf, who was still floating in the air, his hands firmly over his eyes.

"They've gone, Giff!" she called. "Come down!"

But the elf didn't move.

"Giff!" the horse fumed. She turned to Patrice and pawed the ground. "That fool of an elf," she said through gritted teeth, "is going to be the death of me."

"He's probably blocked his ears as well as his eyes, poor thing," said Patrice comfortably. "He can't hear you." She dug in her pocket and pulled out some round white sweets that smelled strongly of peppermint. "Giff!" she shouted. Then, with expert aim, she sent a mint hurtling through the air, hitting the floating elf neatly on the back of the neck.

With a cry of fright Giff threw out his arms and legs, and fell to the ground with a thump. He lay on the grass, his ears quivering with fright. "What hit me?" he quavered.

"Must have been a mosquito, dearie," said Patrice mildly. "Look, the guards have gone. Now we've got to go, too. It's not safe out here. We have to decide what we're going to do."

Giff's ears drooped even more. He beat his fists on the grass. "What's the point?" he wailed. "The plan's in ruins. We failed. Completely, absolutely, utterly. We're doomed!"

"Well, if we're doomed," snorted Maybelle, "let's at least be doomed inside. Come on!"

Giff stumbled to his feet, sniffing, but Jessie stood her ground. She'd had enough of this. "I'm not going anywhere until you tell me what's going on!" she said firmly. She turned to Maybelle. A horse she might be, but she definitely seemed to be the leader in this group.

"You tell me!" she demanded. "Where am I? What is this place? And what's happening to the hedge that you need magic to fix? And who are the Others? How did I get here?" She took a deep breath. "And the main thing is, how do I get back?"

the magic

Maybelle's eyelids fluttered. She tossed her mane uncomfortably. "Ah . . . we'll go into all that later," she said.

Jessie stamped her foot. "No, we won't!" she insisted. "We'll go into it now!"

Patrice gave a little cough. "I really think we should tell the child everything, Maybelle," she said. "We owe her that much, don't you think?"

Maybelle humphed and tossed her mane again. "All right," she said finally. "All right. But I insist that we go inside. The guards might be back this way, and we simply can't afford to be

51

caught here with her."

"The palace is just along the road a bit," put in Patrice, tucking her arm through Jessie's. "And a cup of hot chocolate wouldn't go astray, would it? We can talk on the way."

Hot chocolate in a palace? Jessie looked at her in wonder. But Giff was licking his lips and Maybelle had already started trotting along the road, so she shrugged her shoulders and let Patrice lead her away.

"It's like this," Patrice began, as they hurried along to catch up with Maybelle. "This hedge, you see, is the border of the Realm. It keeps us safe from the Others."

"Who—" began Jessie. Giff interrupted.

"Trolls!" he panted, his eyes wide with fright. "Trolls and—ogres and—goblins—and dragons—and—giants—and—monsters—and—and—"

"And all sorts of nasties, dearie," Patrice said, nodding. She sighed. "They live in the Outlands, on the other side of the hedge."

"But I thought *we* lived there," said Jessie in surprise.

Patrice shook her head. "Oh no, dearie," she said. "Yours is a quite different world. The Doors to your world open by magic. But the Outlands is part of *this* world. And the Outlands creatures would love to get into the Realm, my word they would. But they can't, you see? The hedge keeps them out."

Ahead of them, Maybelle had slowed to a walk. As Jessie watched, she darted into a grove of tall, pale-leaved trees by the side of the road.

"Come on!" urged Patrice.

They followed Maybelle, and soon Jessie saw that behind the trees rose the turrets and spires of a great golden palace, just like the one in her grandfather's paintings. Light streamed from a vast doorway directly below a row of tall windows that stretched across the front of the palace. Jessie was filled with excitement. She imagined walking in that door like a princess and wished she was wearing proper clothes. A nightdress and bare feet didn't seem right for her first visit to a palace. She wondered if she should put on her cloak.

But to her disappointment the others ignored

the main entrance. Instead, they slipped around the side of the building and led her to a very small door hidden behind some bushes.

"In here," whispered Patrice, producing a key.

A few moments later they were in a narrow hallway, and then a small, snug kitchen. Jessie looked around in surprise. "Is this where they cook the food for the whole palace?" she asked.

Patrice burst out laughing, her little black eyes twinkling. "Oh, hardly, dearie!" she giggled. "The palace kitchens are a hundred times bigger than this. This is just for cooking my own meals in my time off. I'm the palace housekeeper, you know. Used to be nurse to all the palace babies when I was younger. Now, you sit down and I'll make you that hot chocolate." She tied a white apron around her plump waist and began bustling around, getting chocolate and milk and cream, and putting cookies on a plate.

Everything seemed so ordinary that for a moment Jessie quite forgot that she was in a very strange place, with some very strange people, and that she had a lot of questions still to be answered.

Then she caught sight of Maybelle leaning comfortably against the table with her back legs crossed, and remembered. "Why do the ogres and trolls and things even *want* to get into your world?" she asked.

Maybelle gave a bitter snort. "They're a nasty lot through and through, and they just want to destroy every beautiful thing they see," she said. "But apart from that, they want the gold that lies in our riverbeds. They're gold mad!" She sniffed. "And of course," she added casually, "they want me."

"You?" Jessie stared.

"Me, and all my friends and relations," Maybelle said. "They want to use us as slaves to work in their mines. In the dark, underground. Harnessed to carts full of rocks. Huh!" She lifted her head and stared straight ahead. Her words might sound disdainful, but Jessie could see that underneath she was afraid. She felt Patrice gripping her arm. The little woman was afraid, too.

"They won't get in, Maybelle," quavered Giff. "Will they?"

"If the hedge keeps going the way it is, I don't see how we can keep them out," huffed the little horse.

"And that, dearie, is where you come in," sighed Patrice, darting a look at Jessie as she put cups filled to the brim with foaming chocolate drink on the table. "Or where you *would* have come in, if you were who we thought you were."

"I don't understand!" cried Jessie.

"I'm not surprised," snapped Maybelle. She heaved herself away from the table and glared at Patrice. "Let me tell it," she ordered. She cleared her throat.

Jessie sipped her hot chocolate. It was delicious! She took another sip.

"The hedge that protects the Realm," Maybelle began slowly and clearly, "is very powerful. The evil creatures in the Outlands have their own magic. But it isn't strong enough to destroy the hedge. Except once in a blue moon. Every fifty years, to be exact.

"The hedge, you see, is kept strong by magic. It's the same magic that keeps the whole of the

Realm running happily and smoothly. But every fifty years the magic runs out and has to be renewed. And this can only be done by the true Queen, using a spell that only she knows. If the magic isn't renewed, the hedge will crumble away." Maybelle paused. "Do you understand?" she asked abruptly.

Jessie nodded. "Of course I do!" she exclaimed. "And I suppose, from what the soldiers said, and because there's a blue moon in the sky, and because the hedge is dying, that the fifty years are nearly up now."

Giff groaned and buried his nose in his cup. "The mermaids are singing," he whimpered. "I don't know what they've got to sing about."

"The mermaids always gather in the Bay for the renewal," Patrice said, turning to Jessie. "They always sing. They're singing now because they believe, like everyone else, that everything is going to be all right."

"But you don't think so," said Jessie, looking at their worried faces.

Maybelle shook her head slowly. "Today at

dawn it'll be fifty years exactly since the magic was last renewed. Only a few grains are left. There should be enough to last till daybreak. But even now . . ."

"Oh!" cried Patrice, tearing off her apron and banging down her cup. "Oh, I can't stand it! I have to go and see."

"Me too, me too!" wailed Giff.

Maybelle snorted. "We'll all go," she said. "May as well know the worst." She jerked her head at Jessie. "You come with us," she said. "We can't leave you here alone. Someone might come in."

Jessie quickly finished her hot chocolate and then Patrice led the way from the kitchen, through her living room and out into a narrow corridor. The corridor led to some steep stairs, and then to yet another passageway that twisted and turned. The ceiling was very low. Jessie had to bend her head to follow the fat little woman toiling on ahead of her. Behind she could hear Giff panting and snuffling, and the neat clattering of Maybelle's hoofs on the floor.

They seemed to have been walking for a very

long time when finally Patrice stopped. In front of them was what looked like a wooden wall. There was a narrow gap in the wall, from where a board was missing, and through it soft light streamed. Patrice turned and put her finger to her lips, then faced the front again and crept forward, very slowly. She knelt and looked through the hole. The others quickly joined her.

The other side of the wall was covered by a gauzy curtain, but Jessie could see easily through the fine material. She found that she was staring straight into a huge, magnificently decorated room lit with hundreds of candles. Crystal pillars rose, glittering, to the high ceiling. Great windows lined one wall. Jessie realized that these were the windows she had seen when she was looking at the front of the palace. In the middle of the room a beautiful, gentle-looking woman sat on a golden throne. Red hair streamed over her shoulders and down her back, and on her head she wore a silver crown. She seemed to be deep in thought.

Beside the throne a huge, strangely shaped crystal jar, open at the top and the bottom, hung suspended in the air, shining in the candlelight. It was empty except for a few flecks of gold drifting slowly around at the very top. As they watched, one golden fleck began to fall downwards. After a minute or two it slipped from the bottom of the jar, hung in the air for a brief moment, and then disappeared with a tiny flash. The woman on the throne sighed and looked even more worried than before.

The four friends pulled themselves away from the wall and crept a little way back down the corridor so they could talk. Patrice clasped her hands. Her eyes were bright with fear.

"Listen," Jessie began. "Why doesn't the Queen just fix the magic now? She's sitting right beside it. She could just say the spell and . . ."

The other three shook their heads sadly. "Poor Queen Helena can't do anything about it," Patrice told her. "She's not the true Queen. She's a dear, sweet lady, and she's ruled us well and wisely, hasn't she, Giff?"

Giff nodded violently. "A bit soft-hearted, maybe," he said.

Patrice shrugged. "A bit too easily taken in by rogues and scoundrels, that's true. But that hasn't mattered up to now."

"Maybe not," Maybelle rumbled. "But in any case she's not the true Queen. She can't do a thing about the magic. She can't help at all."

"Well, where *is* the true Queen, then?" demanded Jessie. "Where is she? Why isn't she here?"

CHAPTER SIX

The sisters

"I 'll tell you the story," said Maybelle. "Sit down."

Obediently, Jessie slid to the floor of the passageway and leaned against the wall. Giff and Patrice sat down beside her.

"Long ago," Maybelle began, "there were two little princesses in the Realm. One, the elder, would be Queen one day. It was she who learned from her mother the spell that would renew the magic. When the time came, only she would be able to make it work.

"She was beautiful, and willful, and charming, and everyone loved her. Her younger sister,

Helena, was also beautiful and beloved. But she was altogether softer tempered and gentler. A good, obedient child.

"The little princesses grew up together in the palace with their cousin Valda, who was about the same age and looked very like them both. Valda always acted sweet and well-behaved, but she had a cruel streak." Maybelle wrinkled her nose. "Valda was the sort of child who smiled at adults, but pinched and bullied smaller children when the adults weren't looking. You know what I mean."

Jessie nodded. She'd met one or two children like that.

Maybelle went on. "Despite their differences, the three girls played together, did their lessons together, and were like sisters. But all of them knew that Jessica would be Queen one day."

Jessie jumped. "What was that name?" she exclaimed.

Maybelle looked at her in surprise. "Jessica," she repeated. "Our true Queen. The one we were calling when we got you by mistake. Anyway . . . when Jessica was sixteen, a stranger visited the

Realm. He was tall and handsome—and from your world. He had found a Door, the same one you came through. There are many, if you know where to look."

"He loved it here," Giff put in, smiling sadly at the memory.

"So he did," Maybelle said, nodding. "He couldn't stay, because mortals can't survive in the Realm for long. But he visited us many times, over several years. He became friendly with many of the Folk. And every time he came, he went looking for Jessica."

"Everyone could see that they were falling in love," said Patrice, biting her lip. "But no one thought there was any harm in it. No one saw the danger at first. And then—"

"They ran away together," Jessie said slowly. "He took her back to his own world and they got married. His name was Robert Belairs."

They stared at her in surprise. "How do you know that?" asked Giff fearfully.

"Please go on," Jessie said to Maybelle. "Tell me all of it."

"They left on Jessica's twentieth birthday. The day that the magic was renewed by her mother, the Queen, and the blue moon hung in the sky," said Maybelle, still looking at Jessie curiously. "Jessica left a letter for her sister Helena. She said that when the time came, Helena should rule the Realm in her place. She said that though she must now live in the new world she had chosen, she would not forget us."

"She didn't take any of her beautiful clothes, or jewels, or anything," sighed Patrice, wiping her eyes. "She only took the charm bracelet that was hung with all her memories of home. In her letter to Helena she said she'd wear it always. It would stop her memory of the Realm from fading. It would help her to remember that in fifty years from that day she must come back—to renew the magic, anoint Helena's daughter as the next Queen, and keep the Realm safe."

"Oh, there was terrible trouble when the King and Queen found out what had happened," breathed Giff, his eyes wide.

"As you can imagine," said Maybelle dryly. "But

eventually they calmed down and saw that what was done, was done. They issued a proclamation saying that when the time came, Helena should take the throne, as Jessica had asked. And that Helena's child would be Queen after her. Almost everyone thought they were right. The people loved Jessica and were sad that she was gone. But they loved Helena, too."

"Valda wasn't happy, though," interrupted Giff, shivering.

"No." Patrice folded her arms and looked grim. "Valda wasn't happy at all. Valda was very angry. She claimed that Jessica had disgraced the royal family by what she'd done. She said that as Helena was Jessica's sister, she was disgraced, too. And she said that Helena was weak and would bring the Realm to ruin." She frowned. "Ah, she was a nasty, jealous, spiteful piece, that Valda, even as a girl."

"In a word," Maybelle said impatiently, "Valda said that she, Valda, should be anointed Queen in Helena's place. She gathered together some power-hungry, flattering creatures to support her. But she'd shown her true colors too soon. No one really wanted her as Queen."

"Eventually, the King and Queen, and the people, too, lost patience with her. They warned her many times, but she wouldn't stop her troublemaking. Finally, a plot to take Helena's life was discovered. And that was the end. The Queen banished Valda to the Outlands. And she hasn't been heard of since."

Patrice sighed. "So now, instead of three princesses, there was only one. Poor Helena. She was so lonely and afraid. She missed Jessica dreadfully. I remember it well. But in time she fell in love and was married, and took the throne. She had a child, a sweet girl, named Christie. And Helena has been a good Queen to us. A good and happy Queen. Now, though, she is in terrible trouble."

"Jessica said she'd come back," said Maybelle. "But she hasn't. And now evil stalks the Realm. The Doors to your world have been locked. But Helena didn't lock them. Someone else did."

"We three had to steal some of the last magic to force open the Door you came through," whispered Patrice to Jessie, clasping and unclasping her hands. "We were trying to call Jessica one last time. But she didn't come. I think . . . I think she must be dead." Tears welled up in her eyes.

"No!" Jessie grabbed her arm. "No, she isn't dead. She's at home. Jessica's my grandmother. The bracelet really must hold her memories of this place. Because she's lost it. And now she's forgotten what she has to do." She spun around to face Maybelle. "Quickly!" she rushed on. "Get me home! I'll bring Jessica back to you."

Maybelle shook her head. "It's too late," she said. "You can't do anything now. And besides—"

"Jessica!" The cry from the throne room was startling in the silence. Then there were sharp, ringing footsteps on the marble floor, and a tinkling sound that Jessie recognized.

The friends scuttled back along the passage to the curtained wall and peeped into the room beyond. Queen Helena had jumped to her feet and was facing someone they couldn't see. "Oh, Jessica," she was crying. "The magic is ebbing so fast, so fast! It is past midnight. The hedge is dying every moment you delay. And my guards say

69

thousands of trolls are massing on the other side. Our people are becoming afraid. Please, please renew the magic now."

"Oh, the morning will be time enough, dear Helena," yawned another voice. "We have until dawn, after all. Just now I am tired to death. A relaxing bath and a soft bed are all I am planning on for the next few hours." There was a low laugh, and then a woman walked into view.

Jessie gasped.

The woman was small, and beautiful like Helena, with long, golden-red hair. She looked very like one of the great ladies in Robert Belairs' paintings. But her eyes were as cold as green ice, and her mouth was thin and proud. On her shoulder perched a pretty gray kitten that Jessie had seen before. And on her wrist was a bracelet. A charm bracelet, which tinkled as she looked around her, smiling at the room as though she owned it.

"Granny's bracelet!" breathed Jessie. "That woman's got Granny's bracelet!" She made a move to spring through the curtain, but Giff gasped in horror and Patrice grabbed her arm and held her back.

"Be still! Be quiet! She mustn't know you're here!" she hissed, pulling Jessie away from the curtain. "Or you'll disappear, as other people have." She tugged until Jessie moved with her and the others further down the passageway.

When they were far enough away not to be overheard, Jessie twisted around to face them. "Why does Queen Helena call that woman Jessica?" she demanded.

Maybelle curled her lip. "Because that woman says she's Jessica," she snorted. "And Helena believes her, as do most others here. Because she looks like Jessica. Because she came into the Realm at the right time. And because she's wearing Jessica's bracelet. To most people, the bracelet is proof of her identity."

"She stole the bracelet," exclaimed Jessie. "Or rather, her horrible cat stole it for her. He tripped Granny up and made her hurt her wrist so the bracelet had to be taken off. Then he took it and hid it, and waited till he got the chance to move it out of the house. I realize now. I actually saw him

71

carrying it to the secret garden late last night. He was taking it back through the Door, to that woman, so she could pretend to be Granny." She turned to Maybelle. "But who is she?" she urged. "Why is she doing this?"

"We believe she's Valda," said Maybelle. Giff and Patrice nodded solemnly.

"We believe that for all these years of her exile she's been building her power, making her own evil magic, and planning her revenge," the little horse went on. "And now, when the Realm is at its weakest, she's returned to carry out her plan. She stole Jessica's bracelet to take away her Realm memories. And she used her own magic to lock the Doors, in case we tried to bring Jessica back ourselves. Jessica could undo her lock-spell in a moment. But we can't. Not without magic."

She sighed. "But why Valda's pretending to be Jessica, and why she claims she's going to renew the magic, when she knows she can't do it, we don't know. After all, she can't pretend she's Jessica forever. She *can't* renew the magic. In the end, everyone will find out that she's an imposter."

"The trouble is, by then the magic will be gone," muttered Patrice.

"Send me back!" cried Jessie. "Send me back quickly, and I'll bring the real Jessica to you. I will!"

They all looked at her sadly. "We can't," said Maybelle simply. "The Door is locked, and we don't have the magic to open it any more. We're very sorry. But we can't send you back. Ever."

CHAPTER SEVEN

Jessie's plan

Later, Jessie couldn't remember how she'd got back to Patrice's cozy little kitchen. All she remembered was finding herself sitting at the table and crying, while Giff forlornly patted her arm and Patrice fussed around offering her cakes and drinks she couldn't swallow.

Maybelle stood shaking her head. "Sorry," she kept saying. "Very sorry."

"Sorry!" choked Jessie at last. She gave a shuddering sob. "What good's that? I want to go home!" She wiped her eyes with the back of her hand. Giff tremblingly offered her a green-and-white spotted handkerchief, and she took it. "I want to go home," she repeated more firmly.

Patrice clasped her little brown hands. "Oh, we wish we could help," she cried. "We'd do anything to help if we could."

"If only the real Jessica was here," moaned Giff, his drooping ears quivering. "Jessica would know what to do. Jessica would do something. Oh dear, oh dear!"

Jessie looked up. A memory stirred in her mind. She remembered her grandmother's laughing face and her voice: *Don't worry so. All will be well.* They were right. Granny wouldn't have given up. She lifted her chin.

"Well, *I'm* here," she said. "And I'm Jessica's granddaughter." Then she thought of something else. Some other words, spoken in her mother's calm, practical voice: *What we need round here is some common sense.* She raised her head higher. "I'm Jessica's granddaughter," she said, "and I'm Rosemary's daughter, too. And I'm not going to let any nasty old witch take over this place. Or steal my Granny's memory. *Or* stop me from getting home. I'm going to *make* her open the Door for me. And that's that!"

Giff stared at her admiringly.

"Oh, that's the way!" shrilled Patrice. "Oh, she does remind me of Jessica, Maybelle."

"That's as may be," retorted Maybelle. "But it's not as easy as all that. What exactly are you going to do, child, may I ask?"

The others waited expectantly.

"Well . . ." Jessie hesitated. Of course she hadn't the faintest idea. She shivered.

"You're cold!" exclaimed Patrice instantly. "Oh dear. I'll light a fire. And in the meantime . . ." She looked around and spied the old gray cloak lying on a chair by the door. She picked it up and handed it to Jessie. "Here," she said. "Put this on, dearie."

Thankfully, Jessie wrapped the cloak around her. Again she breathed in its warm, homey smell.

And then Giff screamed.

Jessie stared at him in surprise. The little elf was as pale as chalk. He was pointing at her with a shaking finger.

"What's the matter?" she asked.

"It's the cloak," exclaimed Patrice goggle-eyed. "That's what it is! Giff, stop that noise, for goodness sake! You're making my head spin!"

Maybelle moved away from her place in the corner and approached Jessie cautiously. She lifted her lips, felt carefully around, and then pulled at the cloak with her teeth until it fell away from Jessie's shoulders.

Patrice clapped her hands. "Told you!" she shrieked delightedly.

"Did you get this from your grandmother, child?" asked Maybelle, dropping the cloak to the ground.

"My name's Jessie!" Jessie snapped, feeling very ruffled. "And yes, it belongs to Granny. But why did you pull it off?"

"Because it makes you invisible, dearie," giggled Patrice. "You gave us such a fright. Didn't you know?"

Jessie stared. "No," she said blankly. "Invisible? But that's not true, Patrice. I wear it all the time at Blue Moon—I mean, at Granny's place. And

78

there's no way it makes me invisible there."

"Well, it does here," said Maybelle with excitement. She pushed at the cloak with her nose. "My word, a cloak of invisibility! I haven't seen one of these for years."

"Only the royal family have them, Maybelle," said Patrice primly. She gathered the cloak up in her arms and smoothed its folds before handing it back to Jessie with a look of respect in her eyes.

Jessie stared at the soft gray material. Invisible! The word rang in her head. "Do you know where in the palace Valda is staying?" she asked suddenly.

Patrice nodded. "Of course. In Jessica's old bedroom," she said.

"Take me there, then," urged Jessie. "Come on! I've got a plan. I'll explain it to you as we go."

A guard stood outside the bedroom door. The four friends peeped at him cautiously from their hiding place behind a golden statue that stood in a turning of the passageway.

"What if she's already had her bath?" whispered

Patrice. "It's late. She might already be in bed."

"Then we'll have to play it by ear," Jessie whispered back. "Don't worry!" She pulled Granny's cloak around her shoulders and watched as the others blinked. She really was invisible! "Are you sure you want to go through with this?" she asked. "It'll mean trouble for you—afterwards."

"Of course we're sure," Patrice said, nodding. "Let's go."

"Good luck!" added Maybelle.

Giff waggled his ears and patted the air where he thought Jessie might have been.

With a wave that of course Giff and Maybelle couldn't see, Jessie slipped from behind the statue and, with Patrice beside her, walked up the corridor toward the guard. Patrice's shoes clattered on the polished marble floor. Jessie's bare feet made no sound at all. The guard stood staring straight ahead, unblinking and at attention, as they reached his side.

"The Lady will be wanting these," Patrice said to the guard. She showed him the two fluffy white towels she carried in her arms. He nodded and knocked at the door.

"Yes?" called a proud voice.

The guard winked at Patrice and opened the door. Patrice bustled into the room beyond, the invisible Jessie close behind her.

The walls of the bedroom were hung with pale blue curtains that fell to the floor in silky folds. The carpet was white and deliciously soft under Jessie's bare toes. The bedhead was painted with tiny blue and gold flowers to match the bed's silken spread. Through an open door a white marble bathroom could be seen. Jessie looked around her in wonder. It was hard to believe that this was where her grandmother had slept when she was a girl. It really was a room fit for a princess.

The woman they had seen in the throne room was standing in front of a tall mirror in the center of the room. Her red hair hung like a gleaming shawl down her back, and she was wearing a deep purple robe. The gray kitten sat at her feet.

"I brought you some fresh towels, my lady," said Patrice, dropping a deep curtsy.

"I already have towels, Patrice," said the woman coldly. "I had to ask for them earlier. Some silly girl brought them to me. It seemed you couldn't be found."

Patrice bowed her head. "It is my rest day today, my lady," she said.

"Rest day?" The woman's lips curved in a thin smile. "It seems you have all been spoiled while I have been away." She raised her hands to her hair and the charm bracelet on her wrist tinkled. "Helena is a dear girl, but far too soft. We shall see about all that—later."

"Yes, my lady," murmured Patrice, and bobbed another curtsy.

The woman's smile faded. She turned to face Patrice. "Don't think you can fool me with your curtsies and your 'my ladys,' Patrice," she sneered. "I know that you have been trying to cause trouble. You and that creature Maybelle, and the absurd Giff. I have . . . friends . . . who tell me what is going on in the palace."

"Spies, you mean," flashed Patrice, gripping the towels in her arms while her face blushed red.

"Friends," snapped the woman. "Loyal subjects who are pleased to have their true Queen home again."

"You aren't our true Queen," Patrice burst out. "You might fool everyone else, but you don't fool me. You aren't Jessica!"

In the corner Jessie put her hand over her mouth. Oh, not now! Oh, be careful, Patrice, she begged silently.

But the woman in front of the mirror only threw back her head and laughed. "You poor, silly creature. Who am I then?"

"You're Valda," cried Patrice. "I didn't nurse you, Jessica and Helena as babies for nothing. I'd know each one of you if I hadn't seen you for a hundred years. You were mean, spiteful and jealous as a child, Valda, and so you are now." The little servant was shaking with fear, but she stood up proudly.

Valda narrowed her eyes. "You never liked me, Patrice," she spat. "Never! And I didn't like you." She took a step forward, her fist raised. "You say one word to anyone about this and you'll regret it.

You'll regret it till the end of your days. Now get out! *Get out!*"

Patrice scuttled to the door, the towels still clutched in her arms. As she left the room she glanced back once, her small black eyes despairing.

Don't worry, Patrice, thought Jessie grimly. We're going to defeat her. And it's now or never.

the thief

When the door closed again and Valda believed herself to be alone, she turned back to the mirror and touched a finger to her smooth cheek. The gray kitten twined itself about her feet. She smiled.

"When morning comes, my little friend," she murmured to it, "these fools will pay for their treatment of me, for I will be Queen indeed. Jessica lies helpless in the mortal world, with no memory of the Realm. She will not stir to save her people now. The removal of the bracelet has seen to that. A few more hours and the last magic will have gone. The hedge will crumble. And my army from the Outlands will come in. Then the people of the Realm will see what it is to be ruled. They will learn to do exactly what they're told. Or face the consequences."

She smiled again, then turned and went toward the bathroom. Jessie held her breath, her ears straining. She heard the sounds of water running in the marble tub and Valda moving around. She heard the rustle of satin as the purple robe was tossed carelessly to the floor, and the clatter of slippers kicked aside. And then she heard the sound she had been waiting for. The tiny jingling of the charm bracelet as Valda removed it and put it down on the side of the bath before getting into the water. Jessie's heart leaped. She'd been certain that the bath would be the one place where Valda could not keep the bracelet on her wrist. And she'd been right.

Jessie stole to the bathroom door. Valda was lying in a billowing mass of scented, pale blue bubbles. Her hair was wound up in a white towel, her eyes were closed. The charm bracelet lay close beside her shoulder. Jessie held her breath and moved into the room. The white floor was cold and smooth under her feet. She made no sound.

Valda lay still. Jessie stretched out her hand for the bracelet. She took it between two fingers, and began to ease it toward her. And then she snatched it, jingling, from the edge of the bath, and ran for the door.

Valda's eyes flew open. She screamed with rage and grasped the slippery sides of the bath, struggling to get up.

"You're too late!" cried Jessie. "I've got Jessica's bracelet. I'm going to take it back to her, so her memory of the Realm will come back. And you can't stop me!" She threw open the bedroom door and darted out into the hallway. The guard on duty, flabbergasted, looked wildly right and left. He could hear Valda's shrieks of rage. He could hear Jessie's thudding footfalls and the tinkling of the bracelet. But he could see nothing at all.

Jessie pounded on, following the way Patrice had shown her. Sleepy guards and servants spun around gasping as they felt and heard her pass, then jumped as they became aware of Valda's furious shouting in the distance: "Stop her! Stop her!"

Panting, Jessie raced down the wide stairs that led to the ground floor and the main entrance. She could hear heavy feet coming after her now. The great golden doors were standing open. She began to run for them.

"Bar the doors! Quickly! Quickly!" shrilled Valda from the head of the stairs. Jessie glanced behind and saw her stamping in fury, wrapped in her purple robe, her red hair streaming. Dozens of soldiers and servants were thundering around her and down the stairs, running to catch the invisible thief. The guards at the entrance jumped to attention and started to swing the heavy doors shut.

But Jessie was too fast for them. She darted forward and just managed to dash between the doors as they closed. She glimpsed the startled eyes of one guard as he heard her pass. Then she was out in the open air and the doors were crashing shut behind her, and Valda was screaming in rage, "You fools! You fools!"

* * *

Five minutes later, outside the Door where they had first met Jessie, Maybelle raised her head. She heard shouting and the sounds of many running feet, mingled with the distant music of mermaids' song. "Here we go," she said to herself. She lowered her head and began quietly nibbling the grass.

In moments the darkened roadway was alive with lights and people. Valda, black cloak flying, swept along at the head of the Royal Guard, the gray kitten perched on her shoulder. When she saw Maybelle she gasped, then frowned in deadly anger.

"You!" she breathed. "I might have known you'd be mixed up in this." She pointed a trembling finger at Maybelle. "All right! Where is the thief hiding?"

Maybelle raised her head and carefully licked up a piece of grass that was stuck to her bottom lip. "I beg your pardon?" she mumbled, her mouth full.

"Tell me!" Valda ordered. "Or it will be the worse for you!"

Maybelle twitched her ears. "I heard a jingling sound running past me and off up the road a few minutes ago," she said, turning her head to look to the left. "Someone was in an awful hurry. Running so fast I couldn't even see who it was."

"You're lying!" Spitting with rage, Valda whirled around to face the gaping soldiers. "Search!" she commanded. "The thief must be around here somewhere!"

"You're wasting your time," said Maybelle calmly. She crossed her front hoofs and watched with interest as the guards began stamping around the area.

Suddenly there was a pounce, a squeak and a cry of triumph. The guard Loris ran up to Valda, carrying a small, struggling figure under his arm.

"Ah . . ." hissed Valda. "Giff the elf. Giff the coward. And what are you doing out here so late, may I ask?"

"He was hiding in a tree, my lady," growled Loris, holding Giff out to show her. Giff trembled and chattered with fright.

"Tell me, Giff," cooed Valda, her eyes as cold as

green glass, "do you know anything about a thief?"

Giff jumped and squirmed in Loris's hand. His terrified eyes were fixed on Valda's.

"Speak!" snarled Valda. "And speak now. And then I may, I just may, spare your miserable life! If not . . ."

"No!" squeaked Giff. "No, don't hurt me, please. I'll tell! I'll tell!"

Maybelle snorted warningly.

"Ignore the horse," sneered Valda, still holding Giff's gaze. "She can't help you. No one can help you. You know where the thief is, don't you, elf? And you're going to tell me. Otherwise . . . !"

Giff covered his eyes with his hands and burst into tears. "She went through the Door!" he sobbed. "She had magic. She went through the Door!"

"What?" Valda wheeled around to face the hedge, her face a mask of baffled rage.

"Magic? But how . . . ?" She glared at Maybelle. "You thought you'd gain extra time for your sneaking thief by sending us off on a wild goose chase, didn't you?" she shouted. "You lying creature! You . . . !"

She pointed at the hedge. "Open!" she
screamed. There was a sighing sound and a gust of
cold air. And then, in the center of the hedge, an
arched door appeared, shimmering and black.

"Go," said Valda to the kitten on her shoulder.
"Bring the bracelet back to me. Do not fail!"

The creature sprang, hissing, from her shoulder and ran for the Door. It leaped into the blackness with a yowl.

Valda turned back to Maybelle. "So your plan
to deceive me failed," she snarled. "Guards! Tether
this horse and take it back to the palace. In the
morning we will decide what its fate will be. The
elf, too. Put it in chains!"

The guards looked at one another. Some of
them weren't sure they liked this so-called Queen.
They didn't like her frowns, or her cruelty, or her
shouted orders. They didn't understand what was
going on.

"Obey!" shrilled Valda. She watched as the
guards slowly and sullenly did as she asked. She
knew they were unhappy. But that didn't matter

to her. In the morning she would have a proper troop of soldiers: the trolls and ogres who had sworn to obey her in return for gaining entrance to the Realm.

She frowned slightly at the thought of the stolen bracelet. How had the thief obtained a cloak of invisibility? How had the thief managed to open the Door? "Jessica!" Valda said to herself, and her frown deepened. She had thought that she had taken care of Jessica.

Then she raised her head. There was no need to worry. Soon it would be dawn. Then the Realm would be lost to Jessica and her kind forever. Valda smiled. She was too strong and too clever to be defeated now. Look how she had forced that stupid elf to tell her where the thief had gone.

Maybelle, tethered tightly and being led away between two guards, saw the smile. And despite her own trouble, and the pain of the ropes on her neck, she allowed herself a small smile, too.

She remembered Jessie's words as they had hurried through the palace hallways. "Once I've got the bracelet, we'll have to make Valda open the

Door so I can get back to Granny," she had said. "And the only way she'll do that is if she thinks I've gone through first."

"How do we make her think that?" Maybelle had asked. "She'll never believe us if we tell her."

Jessie had laughed. "No," she'd said. "But if she thinks she's *forced* someone to tell her, she'll believe, won't she?"

And then she'd turned to Giff and told him what she wanted him to do.

How angry Valda would be if she knew how she had been tricked. How angry if she had heard, as Maybelle had, the tiny tinkle of the charm bracelet as Jessie followed Valda's gray kitten through the Door that Valda herself had opened.

Maybelle plodded on. Good luck, Jessie, she thought. Good luck—and please hurry!

panic!

J essie ran from the secret garden, the bracelet clutched in her hand. The night was dark and cool, but she didn't think of that. All she thought of was reaching the house, of waking her grandmother, of giving her back the bracelet so her memory would return. Then Granny could get back to the Realm in time to renew the magic.

She saw that the back door of Blue Moon was still open, and saw the shadow of Flynn standing guard. She was nearly there—

And then, like a gray streak, Valda's creature was flying from the trees, tangling in her legs, and

Jessie was falling heavily onto the grass, her cloak twisting around her. And the creature was tearing at her hand with its claws, hissing and spitting, trying to make her give up the bracelet. It wasn't pretending to be a cute and helpless kitten now. It was showing its terrible strength.

"No!" shrieked Jessie desperately. "No!"

Flynn's growl was like rumbling thunder as he sprang. In a single bound he leaped from the doorstep to where Jessie had fallen. And then he was snarling at Valda's creature and beating it back, driving it away into the trees.

Jessie stumbled to her feet. Her wrist and the back of her hand were torn and bleeding, but she still had the bracelet. Behind her she could hear the two animals hissing and fighting. She didn't look back: she knew that Flynn could take care of himself. Her job was to give the bracelet to her grandmother.

The house was very still. Jessie crept to Granny's room and pushed the door open.

"Who is it?" asked a trembling voice. Granny was awake!

Jessie switched on the light. Her grandmother lay in bed, looking very small and pale, her white hair streaming over her shoulders and onto the covers.

"It's only me," whispered Jessie. She ran over to the bed and held out the charm bracelet. "Granny, I've found your bracelet."

"I couldn't sleep," mumbled the old lady. "There's something . . . I know there's something I've forgotten. Very important. So important. But I can't think what it is." She tossed her head on the pillows.

Jessie took Granny's unbandaged wrist gently in her hands. She fastened the bracelet around it with shaking fingers, then stood back.

Her grandmother looked at her for a long moment, and then in her eyes Jessie saw a spark, a light that grew and grew in strength. Granny gasped and struggled up on her pillows. "The Realm!" she panted. "My birthday!" She clasped Jessie's arm. "I . . . I have to get back to the Realm! Jessie . . . I have to renew the magic."

"I know," whispered Jessie. She tugged at her

101

grandmother's arm. "Granny, come with me now. We haven't much time. Valda is in the Realm, and everyone thinks she's you! She's planning to let the hedge die. And Maybelle, Patrice and Giff are in such trouble! You can save them! Oh, please come now. To the Door in the secret garden!"

Her grandmother threw aside the covers and tried desperately to push herself from the bed. But she was so weak! Jessie's heart sank. How would she ever walk all the way down to the secret garden?

Through the window she could see the sky was growing paler. It was nearly dawn!

"We have to hurry!" she said urgently. She put her arms around Granny's shoulders and tried to help her. But when the old woman was finally standing on the floor, Jessie realized it was hopeless. Her grandmother had been in bed too long, and was too frail to make the walk. Gently she pushed her back onto the bed.

"We have to find another way," she said.

Granny looked at her in despair. "I must find a Door," she breathed. "Another Door." She lifted her hand to her forehead and the bracelet jingled on her wrist. "I'm still . . . I can't quite remember everything," she said. "But I'm sure . . . I'm sure there was another way. I'm sure Robert said . . ."

Jessie's heart leaped. "Yes!" she exclaimed. "Wait, Granny. I know. I know!"

She left her grandmother sitting staring after her and rushed from the room, the gray cloak flying behind her. Quietly, quietly, she told herself. If Mum wakes up we'll never be able to explain in time.

She ran on tiptoe to the studio. The painting was standing where she had last seen it. As she picked it up she saw again the card on the back. *For my princess on her birthday. Better to be safe than sorry. All my love, always, Robert.*

Good, careful, practical Robert Belairs. The man who had fallen in love with a fairy princess, but always kept his feet on the ground. Robert had always believed in preparing for the worst. Before he died, he had made for his princess a painting that was a spare key to her old home.

Jessie staggered through the shadowy corridors

of Blue Moon, the painting clutched firmly in her arms. It was heavy, and her injured hand hurt. But she didn't stop until she'd reached her grandmother's room again and had put the painting on the floor.

As her grandmother stared at it, another veil of confusion and forgetfulness lifted from her eyes. She smiled. "Robert!" she breathed, her voice full of love. She reached for Jessie's hand. "I must go," she said.

"Take me with you," urged Jessie. "You need help. I'll help you."

Granny squeezed her fingers. "Leave on the cloak, then," she said. "So Valda will not see you. Are you ready?"

Jessie nodded. She saw her grandmother's green eyes flash. "Open!" said a voice she hardly recognized. And then Granny was gripping her hand even more tightly, and Jessie was shivering in a breath of cool wind. The archway in the painting seemed to grow larger and larger, until it was filling all her sight . . .

And then they were no longer in the bedroom

at Blue Moon. They were somewhere else. Not on the roadway beside the dying hedge, where the dawn was staining the sky golden pink and the blue moon was setting. Not in the forest, where the pale-leaved trees rustled their fear in the mauve light. Not in front of the golden palace, where a crowd of anxious people—fairies, elves, gnomes, pixies, creatures of every shape and sort—had gathered, waiting. But in the throne room, under the light of a thousand candles. Beside the twinkling crystal jar, where one last gold fleck drifted slowly downwards.

"What is the meaning of this?" thundered a voice.

Jessie spun around. In an instant her gaze took in the people around her. Queen Helena, looking terrified, stood with her daughter, Christie. A crowd of guards and finely dressed fairy folk, serious-faced dwarves, elves and pixies, huddled behind her. And in one corner of the room were the bowed figures of Patrice, Maybelle and Giff, wound round with chains.

But right in the center of the huge room stood

another figure. A figure wearing a dress of deepest blue and a crown of gold. Valda. Valda, frowning thunderously, pointing at the frail elderly woman standing motionless and apparently alone, her hand on the crystal jar.

"Who is this old crone who dares to break into my palace!" she shrieked. Her eyes widened. "She is wearing my bracelet!" she choked. "The thief!" She whirled around to face the guards. "Take her away!" she ordered.

The guards hesitated.

"What are you waiting for!" screamed Valda. "Are you afraid? Of a silly old woman? Of a nobody, alone and unprotected? Take her away! I command you!"

Two of the guards reluctantly stepped forward.

Jessie glanced at her grandmother in panic. Her head was bent. The hand that rested on the crystal jar was trembling. Granny needed time. Jessie untied the ribbons that held the cloak around her neck. The cloak dropped to the floor. The people gasped as she appeared before their eyes.

"She's not alone!" shouted Jessie. "And she isn't a nobody! She's . . ."

"Jessica!" The cry echoed through the room. And Patrice was staggering forward, pulling at the chains that bound her, her eyes streaming with tears. "Jessica!"

A great shout rose up from the crowd. The guards fell back. Helena stood as if frozen, her hands pressed to her mouth.

"Absurd!" shrilled Valda. "I am Jessica!" But her voice was full of dread as well as anger.

Jessie glanced fearfully at her grandmother. Granny's eyes were fixed on the last fleck of gold as it drifted slowly, slowly downwards. When it reached the bottom of the jar it would float out into the air and disappear. And then . . .

"Granny, the spell," Jessie urged her. "The words! Say the words!"

Her grandmother turned her head and looked at Jessie. "If only I had more time," she said, her voice very low. "More memories are coming back to me every second. But the words . . . Jessie, I can't remember the words!"

CHAPTER TEN

"Remember . . ."

"She's a fraud!" screeched Valda, her eyes fixed greedily on the drifting gold speck. It had nearly reached the bottom of the jar now. "A thief and a fraud! And if you won't remove her from this chamber, I will!" She strode across the room toward Jessica, her hands, tipped with long, pointed nails, outstretched.

"No!" cried Helena. She sprang and caught Valda around the waist. Valda turned, hissing, and tried to push her away. "Jessica!" sobbed Helena. "Oh, my Queen, my sister! Help us!"

At the sound of her sister's voice, Granny's

green eyes flashed with memory. The bracelet tinkled on her wrist as she stretched out her hand again and began to move it over the crystal. Then softly, softly, she began to sing, a strange, lilting song with words that didn't rhyme: "Blue moon floating, mermaids singing, elves and pixies, tiny horses, dwarves and fairies . . ."

Jessie's heart lurched. She was the only one close enough to hear the words. And she knew them! These were the words she'd heard so often when Granny sang to her at night. For all these years, Granny had been singing the spell!

Granny took a deep breath and closed her eyes. She wasn't sure what came next! Jessie put her arm around her and leaned forward till her lips touched her grandmother's ear: "Wait together, in the silence," she breathed.

Granny's eyes opened again. And this time they were full of light. "Wait together, in the silence," she sang, "waiting for the magic rain. Come down, come down, come down and gather, I the Queen command it now!"

There was a moment's electric silence. Then,

without a sound, the last gold fleck drifted from the crystal jar. It hung in the air, winking, in its last instant of life.

Valda shrieked with triumph. Helena screamed and hugged Christie tight. The candles flickered and dimmed . . .

And then the room blazed. Blazed with golden light. And the crystal jar was twisting and turning in the air, filling to overflowing with millions upon millions of chips of solid sunshine that sprayed out and over the top and showered the amazed people with glittering glory. The gold shot up to the ceiling and beat against the windows like sparks from a thousand fireworks.

In the center of the shimmering, whirling mass of gold stood Jessica. But no longer was she frail and old. Now she was again the Jessica of the paintings—young, lovely and triumphant, holding up her arms, shaking back thick, long hair that was no longer white, but shining red.

Jessie blinked, laughed, stared in amazement, hugged herself with relief. With overwhelming happiness she heard a great roar rising up from the crowd outside the palace, as the people saw the dazzling light and broadly smiling guards swung open the windows to let their cheering in.

With a cry of rage, Valda made a dash for the door. But a row of guards stepped forward to block her way. She spun around and shouted to Jessica.

"Queen Jessica, I am your cousin! Do not harm me. Let me go!"

Jessica stepped forward. "You are my cousin, Valda," she said gravely. "But you are my enemy, too. My enemy, and the enemy of all the Realm." She sighed. "We will not harm you. That is your way, but not ours. We will simply again put you out of our sight." She lifted her hand. "By my power as Queen, in the time of renewal of the magic," she said, "I banish you once more to the Outlands. This time, the magic will hold. Now, go!" She pointed a stern finger. And with a final shriek, Valda dissolved before their eyes and disappeared into the air.

An hour later, Jessie and her grandmother stood by the hedge, which stretched high and glossy green before them. On one side of them stood Helena and her daughter Christie, and on the other stood Patrice, Maybelle and Giff.

"Oh, Jessica, why won't you stay!" begged Helena, with tears in her beautiful eyes. "This is your home! We need you!"

Jessica shook her head. "No," she smiled. "My home is in the world of mortals now. I made that choice long ago, Helena, and I don't regret it. It's brought me so much happiness." She laid her hand on Jessie's arm.

"And you don't need me, Helena," she went on, gently. "You'll go on ruling the Realm as well as ever. And only half an hour ago you saw me anoint Christie as the Queen to come after you. You know I've taught her the words to renew the magic when her turn comes." She smiled at the girl, who smiled shyly back. "So the burden has been lifted from my shoulders, and the future of the Realm is secure."

"You will come and visit, though, won't you?" pleaded Giff. "You or Jessie. Please?"

"Oh, please!" echoed Patrice.

"It might be just as well," Maybelle put in gruffly. She coughed. "For a human, the girl seems to be rather useful."

Jessica smiled again. "Ah well," she said. "We'll see. I feel it would be best for me to keep away. But Jessie's a different matter. And if she wants to, and you're willing . . ."

Helena stepped forward and pressed something into Jessie's hand. "You have done us a great service, Jessie," she said. "We give you this as a token of our love and thanks."

Jessie looked. In her hand was a chain bracelet. A single golden charm hung from it. A heart.

"Every time you visit us," said Helena, "another charm will be added. And this way you will always remember us. The Doors are all open again now, my dear. You will always be welcome. You have only to wish."

Jessica's green eyes warmed as she fastened the bracelet on her granddaughter's wrist. "Jessie will be back," she said. "Oh, yes."

The sisters and friends hugged and kissed each other. Giff was crying openly, and even Maybelle was seen to snort away a tear or two. Then Jessica turned towards the Door. "Open!" she said. The archway appeared, and with a rushing sound she and her grandmother moved through it to the other side.

Rosemary stepped through the doorway into the secret garden. She gasped. Her mother and her daughter were standing there in the center of the lawn, bathed in sunlight. She rubbed her dazzled eyes. For a moment, just for a moment, her mother's long, flowing hair had looked as bright and red as Jessie's. But when she looked again, of course, Jessica's hair was quite white. It must have been a trick of the sunlight, she thought.

"Mum! Jessie! I was so worried about you!" she exclaimed. "Neither of you were in your beds! What possessed you to come out so early? Jessie, Granny should be resting."

"Oh no, Rosemary darling," smiled Granny. "Today's my birthday! And I'm much better now. So much better."

They began walking back to the house. "Mum,

you're . . . you're walking so well! And you've found your bracelet," said Rosemary, noticing the bright gold on her mother's wrist.

"Jessie found it for me," laughed Granny. "And now she's got one of her own."

Rosemary looked at her shrewdly. "Something's happened, hasn't it, Mum?" she said. "You've got that look in your eye like you used to have when I was little."

The charm bracelet tinkled on Granny's wrist. She looked around and sighed contentedly, breathing in the sweet mountain air. "It's a beautiful, beautiful day," she said.

Rosemary stopped. "You're not going to move to town and live with us, Mum, are you?" she said suddenly.

"No, darling," Granny answered. "I'm better here. But I've been thinking. Instead of me coming to live with you, you and Jessie could . . ."

"Oh no!" laughed Rosemary, holding up her hand. "Oh no. We can't move! What about my job? And Jessie's school? What about . . .?"

"Nurse Allie said there were several jobs for

nurses at the hospital here," said Granny. "Good jobs."

"And there's a school here," Jessie put in eagerly. "A good school."

Rosemary regarded them both helplessly. "I'll think about it," she said at last.

Jessie and her grandmother exchanged happy looks. They both knew what her decision would be.

"This has been a wonderful birthday morning," said Granny. "I'll never forget it." She smiled and tapped her bracelet. "Now, I'll never forget it."

Jessie looked at her own bracelet, shining gold against her tanned wrist. "No," she said, thinking of all she'd done and seen, and of all the adventures still to come. "Neither will I."

Fairy Realm

BOOK 2

The flower fairies

CONTENTS

CHAPTER ONE

The Trouble with Magic

J essie stepped through the door in the hedge
that led to the secret garden and gasped in
surprise. There, quietly nibbling at the grass, was
Maybelle, the miniature horse from the fairy
world of the Realm. Maybelle raised her head, and
Jessie saw that the red ribbons in her mane were
dusted with gold flecks of magic that twinkled in
the early-morning sun.

"About time you turned up," the little horse said
grumpily. "I've been hanging around here for ages!"

Jessie stared at her. "Have you?" she gulped at
last.

Maybelle sniffed. "I need to talk to you, and I got tired of waiting for you to come over and see us," she said. "It's been weeks! Have you forgotten all about us?"

"Of course not!" exclaimed Jessie. "It's just that . . . I've been so busy."

Maybelle snorted. Obviously she couldn't imagine how anything could be as important as visiting the Realm.

But Jessie really had been busy. She'd been living at Blue Moon, her grandmother's big old house in the mountains, for six weeks now. There'd been a lot to do in that short time. She'd had to help Rosemary, her mother, pack up their house in the city, ready for the move. Then she'd had to help her unpack their clothes and other belongings and store them in the Blue Moon cupboards. Then the holidays had ended and she'd had to start at her new school.

For six weeks her mind had been full of work, plans and problems. She hadn't forgotten for a moment the amazing adventure that had made her new life possible, or the wonderful beings she'd met in the Realm.

How could she forget?

Six weeks ago, she'd discovered the magic Door to the Realm in the part of the Blue Moon grounds Granny called "the secret garden." She'd found out then that her grandmother, Jessica Belairs, wasn't what she seemed. Granny wasn't an ordinary human grandmother at all, but the true Queen of the Realm, one of the fairy Folk. She had left her world many years ago to marry the human man she loved. Now her sister Helena ruled in her place, but Granny still had her Queenly powers, as Jessie had seen with her own amazed eyes.

But Granny's secret wasn't something she talked about—even to Jessie. And with all the ordinary things Jessie had to think about, the magic world she'd entered through the secret garden had started to seem to her more and more like something in a story she'd read, or a film she'd seen, and less and less like a real place.

In fact, sometimes when she thought about it, she wondered if it had all been a dream. But then she'd look down at her wrist, at the chain bracelet hung with a gold heart charm that had been the Realm's gift to her. And she knew that the Realm had been no dream, and remembered that the bracelet was a promise that any time she wanted to, she could return.

She smiled at Maybelle. "What did you want to talk to me about?" she asked.

Maybelle pawed the grass with her front hoof. "I thought it was about time you came back to see us," she said. "The Realm's got shocking problems at the moment, and we could do with a hand."

"What shocking problems?" demanded Jessie. "Surely you've got all the magic you need now." She pointed. "More than enough, I'd say. You've got it all over your ribbons."

Maybelle snorted irritably and shook her mane so that flecks of gold flew into the air and whirled in the sunbeams. Jessie felt little thrills like tiny electric shocks as some of the shining specks fell on her skin. She shivered and giggled.

Maybelle glared at her. "Now don't you get silly too," she ordered. "I've got enough problems with that in the Realm. That's the trouble with magic.

There always seems to be too much of it, or too little. When you came to the Realm last time, we were running out of it, and thanks to you that problem was solved. But now we've got too much. And that's another problem altogether."

"Too much magic?" Jessie giggled again. She could still feel little thrills of excitement all over her arms and face. "How can there be too much magic?"

Maybelle sighed deeply. "They say it always happens just after the magic is renewed," she said. "There's an explosion of it, see, and then for ages afterwards the dust gets into everything. And everyone," she added darkly. "You should see Giff. That elf is just about uncontrollable. Silly as a wheel. And the flower fairies are worse than he is. They're not terribly sensible at the best of times, in my opinion. But now . . . hopeless!"

Jessie bit her lip to keep her giggles back, and nodded sympathetically.

"But the griffins are the real reason I've come to see you," Maybelle grumbled on. "They're the Queen's pets. And they're supposed to guard the

Realm's treasures. Well, that's fine. Let them guard the treasures. No one's arguing about that. But they're not supposed to get so full of themselves that they take over guarding everything else too. Are they?"

"I suppose not," Jessie murmured.

"I'd give anything for a bit of peace and quiet," Maybelle complained. "I'd like just for once to wake up in the morning without my mane and tail all full of giggling fairies. Just for once to have a quiet bowl of oats for breakfast, or a bit of sugar maybe, without having to fight some griffin to get it." She looked up. "You wouldn't by any chance have some sugar about you at the moment, would you?" she asked hopefully.

"No, sorry," said Jessie. "But I could go up to the house and get you some, if you like. Or some bread. Everything's still on the table from breakfast."

Maybelle licked her lips. "Thanks," she said. "Thanks for the offer. But on the whole I'd rather you just came through to the Realm with me right now and tried to sort the griffins out. You're good with magic. That was obvious last time. So—"

"But I'm *not* good with magic," cried Jessie. "Granny's the one who knows about it. She's the one who renewed the Realm's magic. All I did was bring her to you. And to do that I just used human common sense."

"Well, whatever you used, it worked," Maybelle said, nodding. "And I'd be very grateful if you'd stop arguing with me, and come and do it again!" She pursed her lips and tapped the ground with her hoof, waiting.

Jessie grinned. She really didn't think she'd be able to help Maybelle with her problem. But of course she was dying to have an excuse to visit the Realm again. And it *was* Saturday. There was nothing else she had to do, except clean up after breakfast. Mum and Granny had gone shopping and wouldn't be back for an hour or two. So why not?

That was one of the wonderful things about being at Blue Moon. Mum would never have left her alone in the house even for half an hour back in the city. There was so much freedom here! Peace and quiet, and freedom. Starting at a new school had been hard, but that was a small price to pay for living at Blue Moon.

A beautiful blue-and-black butterfly fluttered towards the rosemary bushes that grew around the small, square lawn of the secret garden. Jessie frowned. There was only one cloud in the clear sky of her life at the moment. And that butterfly had just reminded her of it. Tonight! she thought. The concert! Oh, if only I'd kept my big mouth shut! If only . . .

"Well?" Maybelle's impatient voice broke into her thoughts. "What do you say? Will you come? Will you come and deal with the griffins?"

Jessie tried to put her worries out of her mind. "Of course I will," she said. "I don't know if I can help. But I'd love to come."

"Right, then," said Maybelle with satisfaction. "Let's go!"

Jessie put her hand on the little horse's back and closed her eyes.

"Open!" called Maybelle. Jessie felt the cool breeze on her cheek that meant the magic Door was opening. Then, with a tingling of excitement, she felt herself slipping away from her own world and slipping again into the place where her grandmother had been born, and where she herself had had the biggest adventure of her life. The Realm.

Jessie opened her eyes. She was standing on the pebbly roadway beside the tall, glossy green hedge that marked the border of the fairy world. She turned around. The black arch that was the magic Door was already fading, and in a single blink it had disappeared. Her heart skipped a beat.

"Don't worry, now, will you," said Maybelle. "Things are different round here since the magic came back. You won't have any trouble getting home this time."

Jessie swallowed and nodded. She looked around. Everything looked very much as she remembered. The road, the hedge, the fields, a few trees and bushes. The palace, she knew, was just a little way off, behind a grove of trees.

But there were differences. For one thing, the light was bright, rich and golden. Even more golden than it had been the last time she was here. The leaves of the trees and bushes were rustling and the air was full of sound. A humming, twittering, singing sound. Jessie listened carefully. It wasn't just one sound, she decided. She was hearing thousands upon thousands of sounds that all blended into one.

"They never stop talking these days," grumbled Maybelle, flicking her ears forward. "Morning till night — chatter, chatter, chatter. It's enough to drive a horse crazy." She lifted her head. "Be quiet!" she bellowed.

There was dead silence. Then came a chorus of delighted squeaks and cries. The tree branches thrashed and tossed. And suddenly hundreds of tiny creatures with gossamer wings in every possible shade and color were bursting from their hiding places and swooping, in a giggling, excited cloud, around Jessie's head.

maybelle is disgusted

"Jessie, Jessie, Jessie!" chattered the fairies. Jessie felt their tiny hands brushing her long red hair, twisting it into a hundred tangles. She laughed in delight and held out her arm. Most of the little creatures turned their heads away shyly and went on hovering just out of reach. But five of the more daring ones fluttered lightly onto her fingers and perched there, looking up at her with pretty, mischievous faces.

Jessie stared at them, fascinated. When they were darting and flying around in a crowd the fairies all looked alike to her, but now she could see that each one was different. Just like human beings, she thought.

"They're so beautiful!" she said to Maybelle.

Maybelle shook her mane. Three fairies clinging there were flung, giggling, into the air. "They're all right in their place, I suppose," she grumbled. "But the magic gets them all excited, and then they're a plain nuisance. Especially the five you've got there. They're the youngest, and the worst of the lot. A real gang of troublemakers."

Jessie looked again at the fairies on her fingers. They did seem smaller than the others. Obviously they were the best of friends, for they stood in a row, holding hands, opening and closing their wings. The one perched on her thumb was dark, with black hair and eyes. Her silky dress was purple and her wings were soft green.

"You look like a violet," smiled Jessie.

The fairy giggled, put her hand over her mouth, and glanced around at her friends.

"She *is* Violet," sang the fairy balancing on Jessie's first finger. She had a round face with a pointed chin, flyaway fair hair and a bright yellow dress and wings. Her voice was so tiny that Jessie could hardly hear it. "She's very shy," the yellow fairy said, nodding and smiling. "But I'm not."

"Oh, I can see that," Jessie answered. "And if your friend is Violet, would I be right in thinking you're Daffodil?"

"Yes I am!" squeaked the yellow fairy in delight.

"They're mainly flower fairies around here," said Maybelle, "and a few rainbow ones. They tend to cluster round the Doors, so they can get into your world more easily."

"They really come into our world?" asked Jessie. "But no one ever sees them!"

"Oh, of course they see them," said Maybelle carelessly. "Especially now that the magic has been renewed. There's been a lot of to-ing and fro-ing lately. But most people in your world don't believe in fairies, and don't expect to see them, do they? So they don't notice them. It's as simple as that."

"Sometimes they see us and they say, 'A lot of butterflies about today, aren't there?'" burst out Daffodil. "We fool them!" She squeezed Violet's hand and they both broke into peals of laughter that sounded to Jessie like the ringing of tiny bells.

"We fool them!" echoed the fairy on Daffodil's other side, jumping up and down on her toes. Jessie looked at her closely. She had curly light brown hair. Her soft cheeks were pink, her flounced, frilled dress and curved wings were palest pink too, and a thin green sash was tied around her waist. Rose, thought Jessie. A pink rose.

"Don't you be too cocky, you young fairies," Maybelle warned them. "Don't forget, this is your first season out. There are lots of dangers outside the Doors. You two especially," she added, frowning at the fairies on Jessie's last two fingers.

One of them was dark and short-haired, with a starchy white dress and round yellow wings. The other had a long brown plait and was dressed all in blue.

They had been whispering and giggling together, and now they sighed and looked at each other. "No, Maybelle," they chorused. By the look of their cheeky expressions and rolling eyes, thought Jessie, they had no intention of following the little horse's good advice.

"What are your names?" she asked.

They jumped guiltily and fluttered their wings. "Daisy and Bluebell, miss," they said together.

"Oh, you don't have to call me 'miss,'" exclaimed Jessie, laughing in surprise. "It makes me feel like a teacher at school. Just call me Jessie."

Daisy and Bluebell beamed at her.

"Don't you go encouraging them," urged Maybelle. "They'll start hanging round you, and they'll cause you nothing but trouble."

"I think they're really sweet!" said Jessie. "I don't see how they could cause me any trouble at all!" She winked at the five fairies on her hand. "You're always welcome to visit me," she told them. "Any time you like!"

Maybelle grunted. "Well, don't say I didn't warn you," she said shortly. "Now, are you going to come with me and see about these griffins?"

The fairies had been whispering together. Now Daffodil, who seemed to have been chosen to speak for all of them, fluttered her wings and coughed politely. Jessie bent down to listen to her.

"It's our turn to dance in the ring soon. Would

you come and dance with us . . . Jessie?" the little fairy asked.

Jessie caught her breath. She felt herself blushing. "Oh . . . no . . . I can't do that," she said. She saw Daffodil's face fall and felt sorry. "It's just that I'm not very good at dancing, actually," she stammered.

Daffodil's face cleared. "Oh," she said, nodding wisely. She looked around at the others. "Jessie can't dance," she said loudly. "Remember we learned that some humans are like that?"

All five fairies peered curiously up at Jessie's face. She blushed more deeply.

"You'll be with us," called Daisy. "So you don't have to be shy, Jessie. There's no such thing as not being able to dance here."

"Jessie, come on!" snapped Maybelle. "There are more important things than—"

"Oh, please!" squeaked Daisy, jiggling excitedly.

"Please, please, please!" begged the others. And all the fairies darting around nearby took up the call. "Please, Jessie! Please, please, please!" The golden air rang with their tiny voices. The sound went on and on. Jessie looked around helplessly.

"Quiet!" bellowed Maybelle, swishing her tail.

There was another moment's stunned silence.

"Look, you've got to leave Jessie alone now," the little horse said firmly. "She's got something important to do with me. But I promise I'll bring her along to the dance after that. All right?" The fairies nodded, peeping at her with bright eyes. "All right. Now, scat!" Maybelle snorted violently, so that Violet, Daffodil, Rose, Daisy and Bluebell were blown, somersaulting and shrieking, off Jessie's fingers. "Again! Again!" they begged, jumping up and down in the air.

"Come on," ordered Maybelle, nudging Jessie's arm and moving off. Obediently, Jessie followed her, turning one last time to wave good-bye to the fairies who hovered like a cloud of butterflies behind her.

She was pleased to see that Maybelle was trotting in the direction of the trees that clustered in front of the palace. Maybe she'd see her old friends, Giff the elf and Patrice the palace housekeeper. Maybe she'd even see Queen Helena, who'd promised her a new charm for her bracelet every time she came to the Realm. Still, she thought, I mightn't have time. I don't think Maybelle will let me talk to anyone else till I've dealt with the griffins. Whatever griffins are. And then I've got to go to this dance thing.

Jessie sighed. Imagine running into a problem here just like the one she had at home! Her mind went back to that day in the classroom, in her first week at her new school. She'd still been feeling a bit lost and confused. She'd been sitting at her table with a few other kids, trying not to draw attention to herself, just minding her own business. And then . . .

". . . the spring concert," the teacher, Ms. Hewson, was saying, pushing back her curly hair and adjusting her glasses, "is only six weeks away. Now . . ." She consulted the list in her hand. "The sun. Who would like . . . ?"

Several hands shot up, including two at Jessie's table. "Right then—ah, Sal. You haven't been the sun before, have you? Good. Now—breeze?" More hands shot up. "Yes, Michael. Fine." Ms. Hewson made a note, and beamed. "Rabbits?" There was a groan. No one wanted to be a rabbit. Ms. Hewson sighed and made a note. "Rain? Flowers?" Hands went up all over the classroom.

Jessie looked round in confusion. It must be some sort of concert they had every year. Maybe she'd better volunteer for something. She didn't want Ms. Hewson to think she wasn't willing. And she certainly didn't want to end up being a rabbit.

"Butterfly?" sang Ms. Hewson, looking at the class over her glasses. That sounded okay. Jessie put up her hand. So did Irena Bins, whose family lived in the house next door to Blue Moon. Even though they were neighbors, Irena wasn't particularly friendly. She stuck to her own group and had hardly spoken to Jessie since she started at school.

"Ah, Jessie!" smiled Ms. Hewson. "That's nice. Well, Irena, I think we should give Jessie the part, don't you? You were the butterfly last year."

Irena looked sulky. Obviously she didn't agree.

"There's still the rainbow, Irena," soothed Ms. Hewson. "You'd do that awfully well, I think. Will I put you down for that?"

Irena tossed her glossy ponytail and said nothing.

"It doesn't matter, Ms. Hewson," babbled Jessie, feeling herself growing hot. "I don't mind."

"No, no," pronounced Ms. Hewson firmly. "Fair's fair. And Irena mustn't be a bad sport." She wrote on her pad. "Now. Jessie, butterfly; Irena, rainbow. Who would like to do the moon this year?"

And that was how it had happened. It wasn't until later that Jessie found out what a terrible mistake she'd made.

CHAPTER THREE

Giff's Retreat

J essie folded her arms across her chest as she followed Maybelle into the grove of pale-leaved trees. She was remembering the lunch break that had followed Ms. Hewson's giving out of the parts for the spring concert.

Irena sat on a wooden seat, surrounded by her friends and shooting furious looks in Jessie's direction.

"Don't worry about her!" Sal, who sat at Jessie's table and had been chosen to be the sun, came up to Jessie. "Irena Bins always thinks she should be the star."

Jessie looked at her. She'd liked Sal as soon as she saw her on the first day. She had a really friendly face. There was a gap between her two front teeth, and she had freckles on her nose. Jessie thought she'd be perfect as the sun. She was warm and open, with a big, big smile. And she was smiling now. But her words sent a small chill down Jessie's spine.

"The butterfly isn't the star part, is it?" Jessie asked, as casually as she could.

Sal laughed. "Oh, of course it is," she said. "Didn't you know? Irena did it last year. And she was so stuck up about it, honestly!" She lowered her voice. "On a notice board in her room," she whispered, "she's got a big photograph of herself in her butterfly costume. Her father took the picture. And you know what she's got stuck around it?"

Jessie shook her head.

"Butterflies," said Sal. "Poor dead butterflies. All different kinds she's caught. She doesn't know what sorts of butterflies they are, or anything. She just wants a pretty frame for her own picture.

148

I think she's really off."

Jessie glanced at Irena. She felt a bit guilty for whispering about her with Sal. But since Irena had obviously decided that Jessie was her enemy, maybe it was wise to find out a bit about her.

"She was sure she'd get the part again this year," Sal went on. "She thinks she's so great. But I don't think she's such an amazing dancer, anyway."

The small chill running down Jessie's spine became a stream of ice. "Dancer?" she echoed weakly.

"You're so lucky you can dance," Sal rattled on. "I did ballet for two terms when I was younger, but I was hopeless, and Mum let me stop."

She sighed with satisfaction while Jessie gulped and wondered what on earth she was going to do. "That's why being the sun's good," Sal said. "You just get to stand round at the back holding out your arms. I'd be absolutely petrified if I had to do a dance on my own in front of everyone, like you."

By this time Jessie's heart had sunk to the soles of her shoes. She couldn't dance! She'd never had a single proper ballet lesson. Only some creative-movement-to-music classes at her old school. And the special teacher who'd come in to teach those classes had made it very clear that Jessie's efforts to move her thin arms and legs in time to the music were not a bit creative, let alone graceful. She winced as if she was in pain every time it was Jessie's turn to dance. And of course that made Jessie even more embarrassed and stiff. As the lessons went on, she'd got worse instead of better. Now just the thought of dancing made her freeze up.

The one good thing to come out of that terrible lunch break was that Sal had asked Jessie to come and eat with her and her group under the oak tree at the end of the school yard. After two days of lonely lunches, it was nice to have company. But as Jessie sat with her new friends and listened to the gossip and talk about the play and the parts they were all going to be practicing for the next six weeks, she felt sick.

It was going to be so awful to have to admit she couldn't take the butterfly part after all. She imagined Irena's mouth pursing smugly as she leaned over to whisper behind her hand to the person sitting next to her. She imagined Sal's cheerful face falling in surprise and disappointment.

But as it happened, she didn't have to disappoint Sal. Not like that, anyway. Because when she went in to see Ms. Hewson after school to explain, Ms. Hewson had looked at her over her glasses, smiled very kindly, and refused even to consider letting her give up the butterfly part.

"You don't need to have done ballet to do the dance, Jessie," she said. "It's very, very simple. Most of it you just make up yourself, as you go along. You'll be absolutely fine. All you have to do is move gracefully to the music."

Move gracefully to the music! That was exactly what Jessie couldn't do. And the next few weeks' practices had proved it too.

Everyone else slowly learned their parts. Gradually the play came together. But Jessie, who only had to flutter around and didn't even have to remember proper dance steps, was awkward and shy. Her costume was good. She was wearing a black leotard and tights, and had silver antennae on her head and floating sky-blue wings. But she was a hopeless butterfly. She knew it, and so did everyone else.

"That was very nice, Jessie. You look beautiful. But on the night, just try to forget yourself and move with the music," Ms. Hewson had said after Friday's dress rehearsal, the last before the concert on Saturday night. "Just think, 'I'm a beautiful, graceful butterfly,' and enjoy yourself!" She said the same thing every time, and she always said it kindly, with a smile on her face. But Jessie could tell she was terribly disappointed and worried.

"That Jessie dances more like a stick insect than a butterfly, if you ask me," Irena Bins muttered to one of her friends. "She'll ruin the whole thing!"

"Your costume is so lovely," said Sal loyally, as they walked home. "Who made your wings?"

"My grandmother made them for my mother when she was a fairy in a play years ago," Jessie answered.

She remembered how Granny had gone looking for the wings and found them in an old chest of drawers in the storeroom, wrapped in tissue paper. She remembered how Granny had smiled as she handed them to her. "Your mother always loved to dance," she said. "And so did I. We're so proud of you, Jessie."

After that, Jessie just couldn't tell her how she felt. But tonight Granny would see what a bad dancer she was. And so would Mum. And everyone else. Irena Bins was right. Jessie would ruin the whole spring concert.

No wonder the brightness of her first weeks in her new home had been clouded. No wonder she hadn't even tried to visit the Realm again. Even now, walking on its soft grass, breathing in its golden air, the thought of the play was filling her mind and stopping her from enjoying herself.

"Oh dear," sighed Jessie aloud.

Maybelle stopped and looked around at her. "What's up with you?" she inquired.

"It's just . . . oh, nothing," said Jessie. She looked ahead, and her heart gave a skip as she saw Queen Helena's golden palace shining between the trees. She'd been so busy thinking that she hadn't noticed where Maybelle was leading her.

"Are we going to the palace?" she asked hopefully. Suddenly she'd had a marvelous idea. She would ask Queen Helena to help her with the butterfly dance. Perhaps the Queen could put some sort of spell on her.

Maybelle shook her head. "Not the palace itself. Round the back," she said. "The food storehouse. First things first, I say. We're nearly there. Just around this—" She jumped violently as there was a sharp explosion above their heads.

"Look out below!" squeaked a voice from the trees. "Oh no! *E-e-eek!*"

There was a smashing, cracking sound. A shrieking bundle of green, a trailing rope, bells, streamers, a mosquito net, an old shawl, a sun hat, a rusty door-knocker and two broken shopping baskets crashed to the ground.

Jessie and Maybelle jumped aside just in time.

"Giff!" roared Maybelle at the groaning green heap lying in the mess on the ground beside them. "What on earth do you think you're playing at? You could have crushed us to smithereens."

Giff the elf sat up slowly, his long, pointed

154

ears bent nearly double. In one hand he held a piece of string to which was tied a tattered bit of green rubber. In the other he held a notice. *Giff's Retreat*, it read.

He looked at the notice and began to cry. "Oh, my beautiful new house," he wept. "It's ruined! That stupid balloon . . ."

"What new house?" shouted Maybelle. "Giff, you absurd elf, why are you making a new house? You've got a nice house already."

Giff wiped his nose with a green-spotted handkerchief and stood up. "Haven't you heard?" he sniffed. "A griffin's decided to guard my house. And it won't let me in. I've been sleeping on Patrice's couch for three days, waiting for it to go, but it won't. So I decided . . ." Then he noticed Jessie. "Jessie!" he squealed. He dropped the string and the notice and flew into her arms.

Jessie laughed. It was so good to see him!

Giff started to tell her about the house he'd been trying to build. A griffin was guarding the hardware storehouse, he said, so he hadn't been able to get any nails or proper wood or anything. But he'd gathered a few bits and pieces from Patrice's junk room, and he'd planned to make a really sweet little house out of those. It was to be suspended by a balloon, right at the top of a tree. His plans had worked perfectly—at first. But then he'd decided to nail his *Giff's Retreat* sign to the balloon. Things went from bad to worse after that.

"Poor Giff!" said Jessie, shaking her head and trying not to let him see her smile.

Giff snuffled again. "So I *still* haven't anywhere to live," he moaned. "And I'm tired of sleeping on Patrice's couch. It's got lumps! And Maybelle doesn't care. She doesn't care that I'm homeless. She doesn't care that the griffins—"

"I'll have you know, Giff," Maybelle broke in sternly, "that I've brought Jessie to the Realm especially to do something about the griffins. We're going to the food storehouse first. If you want to come with us, come. If you don't, stay where you are. Just don't hold us up. There've been enough delays already!"

Giff meekly took Jessie's hand and the three friends trudged on through the trees until they reached the palace. As they began walking around to the back of the building, Jessie remembered what she'd been thinking about before Giff had dropped so surprisingly out of the sky.

"Maybelle, could I see Queen Helena, do you think?" she said. "I've got something to ask her."

The little horse grunted. "Sorry, didn't I tell you?" she answered. "Queen Helena's off traveling with the King and Princess Christie—visiting the people and creatures in all the different parts of the Realm. Celebrating the renewal of the magic. That's the whole point, you see. The griffins wouldn't be a problem if it wasn't for that. Queen Helena can manage them. They are her pets, after all."

Jessie felt bitterly disappointed. What bad luck! Queen Helena could have helped her with her butterfly dance. She was sure of that.

They pushed through some bushes and came out behind the palace and in front of a tall, round building made of stone. Suddenly there was a deafening, screeching roar. And in an instant Jessie had forgotten all about school, and Ms. Hewson, and Irena Bins. And she'd forgotten about the butterfly dance.

Because she was staring straight at the slashing claws and wicked curved beak of a huge, angry, winged monster.

CHAPTER FOUR

The Griffin

Jessie screamed. Giff screamed. Even Maybelle snuffled through her nose in shock and took a quick step backward. "Run for the bushes!" she ordered. "It won't follow us there."

They scuttled back to the shelter of the bushes beside the palace and crouched there, panting.

"What is it?" cried Jessie, peering out in horror at the savage creature lumbering backward and forward in front of the storehouse, flapping its wings, lashing its tail and snapping its beak. Its back legs and tail were like a lion's. But its head and claws were those of a huge eagle.

Maybelle stared at her. "You know what that is, Jessie. What's the matter with you? That's a griffin."

"*That's* a griffin?" Jessie exclaimed. "But . . . but it's *horrible*. It's *terrifying*! It . . . it wants to *eat* us!"

"Yes," agreed Maybelle calmly. "That's the trouble with griffins."

"But you told me they were Queen Helena's *pets*!" Jessie shook her head. "No, no. I'm sorry, but I can't help you after all." She caught sight of Giff's surprised and disappointed face. "I—I was expecting something . . . smaller," she explained. "Something without a terrible beak and claws. And with a nicer nature."

"Well, if they were smaller and weren't so nasty we could deal with them ourselves, Jessie," snapped Maybelle.

"Or even if there weren't so *many* of them," added Giff gloomily.

"How many are there?" asked Jessie, staring in fascinated horror at the creature, which was now sitting scratching like a dog.

"Four," sighed Maybelle. "There were two, but

they had twin griffinettes a couple of years ago. And Queen Helena, well, she's so soft-hearted . . ."

"Too soft-hearted!" snuffled Giff.

"Yes, well, maybe. Anyway, she couldn't bring herself to give the griffinettes away, so she kept them. And now they're almost as big as their parents, and just as much trouble."

"Psst!" The piercing whisper right behind her ear nearly made Jessie jump out of her skin. She twisted around quickly to meet the black button eyes and plump face of Patrice, the palace housekeeper.

"Jessie," exclaimed Patrice, "what on earth are you doing here?" She turned and frowned at Maybelle. "You brought her, didn't you?" she demanded, shaking her finger at the tiny horse.

Maybelle flicked her tail. "Someone had to do something!" she snorted. "I need my oats."

"Oh, you and your oats!" hissed Patrice, glancing nervously at the griffin. "At least you can eat grass. What about food for everyone else? And what about the hardware storehouse? No one can build anything, or make anything.

163

And what about Giff's house?"

"Yes! What about that?" echoed Giff mournfully.

Maybelle wrinkled her nose and huffed. "Oh yes, all that too," she said.

Over by the food storehouse, the griffin grumbled to itself and settled down by the door. But its glowing eyes still darted suspiciously around, watching for the slightest movement.

"Let me get this straight," said Jessie. "There are four griffins. One's here, at the food storehouse. One's at the hardware storehouse. And one's at Giff's house. Where's the other one?"

"It's at the treasure house, where it belongs," said Patrice. "Where they *all* belong. They've gone crazy with all this magic in the air, and they've decided between themselves that they're not all needed at the treasure house any more. So three of them have gone off and found other places to guard. That's all griffins know about—guarding things. No one can reason with them."

"No one ever could, except Queen Helena," said Maybelle gloomily.

"Well, you'll have to send for her, then," said Jessie reasonably. "She'll have to come back from her trip."

"She can't!" moaned Patrice, twisting her apron. "She's only halfway around the Realm. The magic's just been renewed. It's a great celebration here. She can't disappoint half her subjects like that."

"Well, she'll be pretty disappointed herself if she comes back and finds that everyone at home's dead of hunger or been eaten by griffins, won't she?" Jessie pointed out. "I really think you'd better send for her."

"It's just . . ." Maybelle rolled her eyes and sighed. "It's just that I thought maybe you could think of a way to save us having to do that. We hate to worry her. Still, if you won't . . ."

"It's not that I won't!" exclaimed Jessie, more loudly than she'd meant. She saw the griffin turn its fiery gaze toward the bushes. She lowered her voice. "It's not that I won't. It's that I *can't*, Maybelle."

Maybelle sighed again. And Giff sighed too. His ears were drooping nearly down to his shoulders.

Jessie bit her lip. "Look," she said. "I'll think about it. Maybe I can come up with some plan or other."

"Jessie, Jessie, Jessie!" sang dozens of tiny, tinkling voices from the grove of trees behind them. Maybelle groaned. "Not those pests again," she muttered.

A crowd of fairies flew out from their shelter, hovered over Jessie's head for a moment and then darted off, laughing. They were heading straight for the griffin.

The beast raised its terrible eyes to look at the delicate creatures fluttering around its head. Jessie clapped her hand over her mouth. "Oh! Look out!" she called.

Patrice beamed. "Don't fret, dearie. The griffins won't touch the flower fairies. I think they sort of like them, really. If griffins can like anyone."

"Jessie, Jessie, Jessie," chorused the fairies, leaping in the air and bouncing on the griffin's wings. "Come on! Come on! Come on!"

"Pests!" snapped Maybelle.

"Dear little things," smiled Patrice. "Do they

want you to dance with them, Jessie? I'll bet they do. They miss Queen Helena and Christie terribly, poor loves."

Jessie squirmed uncomfortably. "I can't dance, Patrice. They wouldn't have any fun dancing with me. They'd just be embarrassed."

"Oh, I wouldn't worry about that," said Patrice. "I don't think flower fairies know how to be embarrassed. They'll have plenty of fun." She looked sharply into Jessie's face. "You look as though you could do with a bit of fun yourself," she added. "You feeling a bit peaky?"

Jessie shook her head. She didn't want to talk about her problem. Not now.

"Well," said Patrice, after a moment, "there's not much point in hiding out here, is there? If you're going to do some thinking, dearie, you may as well come into the palace and do it there. Besides, if you're going to dance with the little ones afterward, we'll have to go to Queen Helena's bedroom so I can get you some wings."

Jessie's eyes widened. "Wings?" she exclaimed.

"A waste of time," snorted Maybelle.

"Nonsense," Patrice snorted back. "For all you know, Maybelle, the dancing will help Jessie think. Stir up her brains, or something."

"Or something," repeated Giff, nodding eagerly.

"Follow me," said Patrice.

Giff slipped his hand into Jessie's. "Do you think the dance will really stir up your brains?" he asked.

Jessie had to smile. "I hope so, Giff," she said. She turned to follow Patrice and Maybelle. All the time one word was ringing in her ears. *Wings*.

Jessie stood, amazed, in the center of Queen Helena's beautiful bedroom. It was large and light. Long, transparent curtains billowed at the windows. The soft white carpet was scattered with tiny yellow flowers and green leaves.

But it wasn't the pretty carpet or the delicate furniture that Jessie was gasping at now. She was staring at Patrice, who had opened a large carved chest at the end of the bed and was carefully laying out its contents on the yellow silk bedcover.

Wings. Shining, shimmering wings.

"Come closer, dearie," called Patrice, beckoning. "You'd better choose for yourself."

Jessie tiptoed over to the bed. The wings lay spread out on the yellow silk. They looked as if they would tear at the slightest touch.

"Oh, I don't think I should," Jessie stammered. "Queen Helena wouldn't like it. They look so precious."

"They are precious," Patrice agreed, smoothing a fold from the edge of a wing with one gentle brown finger. "But they're stronger than they look, dearie. You won't hurt them. And I know Queen Helena would want you to borrow a pair. She'd love the idea of the flower fairies having a big person to dance with while she's away. They do adore it, bless their hearts. And none of the Folk here will dance without Helena, you see. It's not done. It's bad manners, in the Realm."

"But it would be all right for me?" asked Jessie.

"Oh, yes, of course! Because you're a human, aren't you, dearie? The rules don't apply to you. Now. Which pair would you like?"

CHAPTER FIVE

The plan

J essie looked carefully at the wings. There were
dozens of them, and they were all different.
She saw that they were exactly the same shape as
the ones her grandmother had given her for the
butterfly dance. But Granny's wings had been
hemmed on the sewing machine and made of ordinary silk. These seemed to have been made with
no thread at all, and the material was like nothing
Jessie had ever seen or felt. They were all so beautiful! It was impossible to choose between them.

"I have some wings at home that Granny
made," she said, her eyes darting from one glorious

color to the next. "They're the same shape as these. But . . ."

Patrice's button eyes softened. "Ah, yes," she said. "Well, of course your grandmother would have remembered the design, wouldn't she? She'd have chosen from this chest of wings many times, as a girl. The Folk always wear them when they dance with the flower and rainbow fairies. And your grandmother danced often. She was a princess, remember. The princess who was going to be Queen one day. Besides, she adored dancing." Again the plump little housekeeper smoothed a wing lovingly.

"But she couldn't make wings like these in your world, dearie," she explained. "To make wings like these you need Realm magic. As I said, they're precious."

Precious. Jessie stood quite still, staring at the wings. She'd had an idea. An idea that might solve all the Realm's problems with the griffins. She thought about it with growing excitement. It just might work! It was certainly worth a try.

"Come on, Jessie," urged Patrice. "You have to

choose. Maybelle will be having conniptions in my kitchen if we don't get on. The best rule, they say, is to choose the wings you feel are most like you."

Jessie decided not to say anything to Patrice about her idea yet. She'd wait until she could talk to Maybelle as well.

But before she could do that, she had to make a choice. She looked over all the wings again. Her hand stretched out and hovered over a yellow pair that shimmered pink at the edges like a rose, or a sunset. Then it moved to a creamy white pair that shone blue and purple and green like the inside of a shell as it caught the light. Still she hesitated.

Her eyes moved over the rich colors. Pink, lilac, soft grey with silver stars, rich purple veined and edged in gold, buttery yellow, palest green . . . And then she saw them, over on one side. Her wings. Pure sky blue, deepening to richer blue at the bottom, fading to lilac at the top. Very like the ones Granny had made for Mum all those years ago. She pointed. "I'll have those, please," she said.

Patrice beamed. "They were your grandmother's favorite," she said. "She wore these far more than any of the others. Isn't it lovely that you chose those?" She picked up the wings. "Turn around, dearie, and I'll put them on for you."

Jessie turned around as Patrice fastened the center of the shining wings to the back of her top, and slipped the fine bands at the tips around each of her wrists. She was glad she had worn a skirt today instead of jeans. She raised her arms and gasped with pleasure as the movement made the wings flutter around her. They felt wonderful. They made her feel quite different. Lighter than air. She spun round to look at herself in the long mirror that stood by the windows.

"That's the way, dearie," said Patrice with an approving look. "Now . . ."

But then Jessie squeaked with shock. She was staring at the mirror. "P-Patrice!" she stuttered. "L-look at me!"

Patrice frowned slightly. "Something wrong?" she asked.

Jessie raised her arms again, her mouth gaping, her eyes wide with excitement as she watched her reflection. The beautiful blue wings were shimmering behind her, her skirt billowed in the breeze from the open windows, her long red hair was lifting and falling, and her feet—her feet were trailing high above the carpet!

"Patrice," she gasped. "I'm floating! Patrice! I'm . . . I'm flying!"

Patrice laughed. "Of course, dearie," she said. "What did you expect?"

In a happy dream Jessie half walked, half flew back to Patrice's cozy kitchen on the ground floor of the palace.

Maybelle and Giff were waiting for her impatiently.

"At last!" exclaimed Maybelle. She watched Jessie turning and twisting in the air and huffed crossly. "Now she's gone silly!" she complained to Patrice. "She'll be no use whatever to us now, thanks to you."

"Oh, never mind all that," smiled Patrice, getting out some glasses and putting ice into them. "Doesn't she remind you of her grandmother? See, she chose the wings Jessica used to wear. Isn't that lovely?"

Giff sniffled. "Lovely," he repeated. He pulled out his handkerchief and blew his nose. "It makes me sad."

"It makes me happy!" cried Jessie, spinning around the kitchen table.

Maybelle tapped her hoof on the floor. "Any thoughts on the griffin question?" she inquired.

Jessie stopped sailing around the room. In the excitement of flying, she'd actually forgotten all about her idea and the griffins! She sat down at the table. "I have had a thought, actually," she said.

Patrice put a tall, frosted glass of rosy pink drink in front of her. "I don't have any chocolate left, dearie," she said. "I was going to try to bully that griffin into letting me get some, and a few other things I'm out of, when I bumped into you. So I can't make you hot chocolate like last time. But I think you'll like this. Have a taste."

Jessie sipped. The drink was wonderful! It was—well, she didn't know how to describe the taste. It was cool, and very refreshing. It wasn't sour and it wasn't sugary. It was a bit like raspberry lemonade might be, but without the fizz. And it left a tingle on her tongue after she'd swallowed, like sherbet did. She licked her lips and took another drink.

"Your idea!" urged Maybelle. "Tell!"

"The griffins' proper job is to guard the treasure house. Right?" Jessie began.

Giff nodded violently and gulped his drink.

"But because they've been affected by all the magic floating around, they've suddenly decided that only one of them is really needed to guard the treasure house," Jessie went on. "So that means that three of them are free to go off and find other places to guard. They don't care that no one wants them to. All they know is that their job is to guard things, so they find whatever they can that looks important and they guard that."

"We know!" groaned Giff. "We know!"

"My idea," said Jessie slowly, "is to persuade the griffins that they're all needed back at the treasure house. Then they'll leave the other places alone."

"How will we do that, though?" asked Patrice anxiously. "How do we persuade them?"

"Simple. We let them know that something very precious to Queen Helena has to be guarded," said Jessie. "Something that's not usually kept in the treasure house but is about to be moved there."

"Something precious?" asked Giff. "What do we have that's precious?"

"The wings," said Jessie. "Queen Helena's chest of wings."

There was a short silence. Maybelle, Patrice and Giff looked at one another. Then Maybelle spoke. "It could work, you know," she said. "Everyone knows how much Queen Helena cares about the wings. Even the griffins know. But the problem is, how do we get close enough to them to make them understand? They just screech and carry on as soon as they see us."

"I've thought of that, too," said Jessie.

They listened carefully while she explained. And then they began to smile.

At the Treasure House

The treasure house wasn't really a house at all, Jessie found. It was an underground room at one side of the palace. All you could see above the ground was a huge flat stone covered with strange carvings. On each side of the stone was a small tree with red leaves. And on top of the stone crouched a fearsome-looking griffin.

"It's much bigger than the one guarding the food storehouse," whispered Jessie nervously, peering out at it from the corner of the palace building.

"Oh yes," Patrice said, nodding. "It's the daddy

of the family. Huge, isn't it?"

"Huge!" echoed Giff, twisting his handkerchief.

Jessie glanced behind her at the two rows of palace guards waiting there with the chest of wings. They were standing at attention, in full uniform, but their faces were worried.

"Get ready," she breathed. The leader nodded.

Jessie looked down at her hand, where Violet, Daffodil, Rose, Daisy and Bluebell were jumping up and down with impatience.

"Okay?" she whispered. "Remember everything?" The fairies nodded.

"Go, then," said Jessie, raising her hand. And immediately the five tiny figures darted from her fingers and sped, chattering and laughing, to perch on one of the red trees right beside the griffin's left ear.

The griffin raised its head and rumbled thoughtfully in its throat, but made no attempt to scare the fairies away.

"Did you hear about Queen Helena's precious chest of wings?" squeaked Daisy at the top of her voice. "Did you hear that it has to be moved from her room because the room is to be painted?"

"Yes! I heard!" shouted Bluebell. "But, um, oh dear, Daisy! I'm *so-o* worried. The wings are Queen Helena's *greatest* treasure. However are they going to be kept safe *now*?"

Jessie covered her face with her hands. "Oh no," she said in a low voice. "I'm not sure this is going to work. The fairies aren't very good at acting, are they?"

Maybelle snorted. "Don't worry about that," she said. "Griffins are pretty stupid. Look, it's listening to them."

Sure enough, the griffin had turned its head toward the fairies.

"Before she went away, Queen Helena told the guards that when the time came they had to bring the wings here, to the treasure house," said Daffodil, loudly and slowly. "She thought that there would be *four* strong griffins to guard them here, and they would be safe. But only *one* griffin is here to guard them now. And if an enemy comes . . ."

There was silence. Jessie saw Daffodil dig Rose sharply in the ribs. Rose jumped. "Oh," she shrieked. "Oh, yes, um . . . If an *enemy* comes, *one* griffin might not be enough. And if even a *single* pair of wings is stolen, poor Queen Helena will be so, *so* unhappy."

The griffin stayed quite still. Its brow wrinkled. It looked as though it was thinking about what the fairies had said—although, Jessie admitted to herself, it was hard to tell. It could just have had a pain in the stomach.

Violet clasped her hands and took a deep breath. "I wish *all* the griffins were here to guard the wings," she bellowed. "Don't you?"

"Oh yes, yes!" shouted all the fairies together. "If only *all* the griffins were here to guard the chest of wings! Then it would be safe, just as Queen Helena had planned."

Daffodil cupped her hand around her ear. "Listen!" she yelled. "I think I can hear some guards coming with the chest right now!"

Jessie crossed her fingers. She turned to the leader of the guards and gave a signal.

At a nod from their leader, four of the guards picked up the chest by its handles. The others formed lines on either side. Then they smartly marched around the corner of the palace, toward the treasure house.

As soon as it saw them, the griffin sprang to its feet, its red eyes blazing.

The leader of the guards cleared her throat and stepped forward, spreading out a paper she held in her hand.

"By order, a chest of wings to be placed for safety in the royal treasure house," she read in a ringing voice, and flung open the chest to show its glimmering contents.

The griffin glared. It held the guard's gaze for a long moment. Then it threw back its head and let forth a blood-curdling shriek. The red trees quivered and a few leaves fell to the ground. The five flower fairies clung desperately to their perches. The guards rocked back on their heels in shock but stood their ground.

Jessie grabbed Patrice's hand.

"It's going to eat the guards," moaned Giff. "Oh it is, I know it!"

The griffin screeched again. And this time its

call was answered. From three different places.

"It's calling its family!" Maybelle burst out in a piercing whisper.

A terrifying rush of sound filled their ears. They looked up. The three other griffins were flying toward the treasure house, their wings beating the air, their sharp curved beaks gaping open. They wheeled in the air and plunged earth-ward, landing beside the flat stone.

Now the guards were facing four angry-looking creatures. Still they held their ground, standing to attention around the precious chest.

The father griffin moved slowly from the top of the flat stone. It fixed the head guard with a steady, serious gaze, and sat down deliberately in front of one of the red trees. The biggest of the other griffins lumbered over to join it. The other two took up their positions on the opposite side.

The head guard saluted. Only a slight sheen of sweat on her top lip showed how nervous she was. She shut the lid of the chest and pointed at the flat stone, murmuring some words Jessie couldn't hear.

With a grating sound the stone slid backward,

revealing a wide, steep stairway. The leader of the guards nodded, and the four guards carrying the chest stepped forward. Followed by their leader, they marched to the stairway and then, slowly and carefully, began to ease the chest down the stairs into the darkness below. After a few moments the sounds of their footsteps died away. The griffins sat as still as if they were carved in stone.

In the ten minutes it took for the guards to return, Jessie, Patrice and Giff gripped one another's hands in silence. Even the flower fairies were still and watchful. The guards remaining by the treasure house stood to attention, looking straight ahead.

At last, to Jessie's enormous relief, they heard again the sound of footsteps on the stairs. The five guards climbed back up into the sunlight, blinking. Without looking at the griffins, they marched briskly across the grass to join the rest of the troop, while behind them the stone slid slowly back into position.

Jessie breathed out. It seemed to her that she'd been holding her breath for a very long time.

The head guard faced the griffins once more. "Guard Her Majesty's treasure well," she said loudly. "Her happiness, and that of the Folk of the Realm, now depends on you."

She spun around to her troops. "About face! Forward march!" she ordered. And gladly the guards turned and marched away from the fearsome creatures whose stonelike stillness had somehow started to seem even scarier than their growling.

When the guards had rounded the corner, the griffins sat silently for a moment longer. Then in one movement they all lay down. Still they made no sound, but their red eyes were fierce and watchful. They didn't look up as the flower fairies fluttered from their places and flew off. They didn't scratch, or twitch an eyelid, or move a muscle. They just crouched, on guard.

"Mission accomplished," muttered the head guard as she marched her troops past Patrice, Maybelle, Giff and Jessie. "See you back at the palace."

"We did it, we did it!" twittered the fairies,

landing on Jessie's shoulder.

Jessie peeped out at the motionless griffins. "They should be all right from now on, don't you think?" she asked Maybelle.

"I'd say so," replied the little horse. "They look much more normal now. That was quite a good idea of yours. I'm surprised I didn't think of it myself."

"*Quite* a good idea?" exclaimed Patrice. "It was brilliant!" She clapped her hands. "Now I can stock up on food again."

Giff nodded. "Brilliant!" he said. "Now I can get back into my house."

"And I," snuffled Maybelle, "can get a bowl of oats in peace."

"And Jessie," squeaked a tiny voice in Jessie's ear, "can come and dance with us! Can't you, Jessie?"

Jessie giggled as she felt Daffodil's tiny hand plucking at her hair. She raised her arms. She felt her wings billow around her and her feet lift from the ground. "Yes," she laughed. "I can."

❊ ❊ ❊

Jessie would never forget her first dance with the flower fairies of the Realm. In the center of a ring of tall trees, with Violet, Daffodil, Rose, Daisy and Bluebell close beside her and hundreds of other delicate winged creatures moving around her, she floated, spun and swayed to music that seemed to come out of the golden air.

Soaring in the blue between the treetops, or springing on the grassy ground, she danced, for the first time since she was very, very small, without thinking about what she was doing. It was the wings that made the difference, she thought. Because they were making her lighter than air, she could forget all about stumbling or being stiff and shy. The music seemed to become part of her, filling her mind, and making her arms, hands and feet move of their own accord. It was a wonderful feeling.

"That was so lovely!" she sighed to Patrice after the music had finally drifted into silence and the fairies, chattering and waving, had flown back to the trees to rest. "That was . . . I suppose that was just like dancing's supposed to be. Oh, I wish . . .

I wish I could borrow these wings. Just for tonight. I've got to dance at my school concert. The wings would help so much!"

She glanced at the little housekeeper's thoughtful face. "Don't worry, Patrice. I know it's impossible," she added quickly.

Patrice cupped her chin in a small, plump hand and winked. "Nothing's impossible, dearie," she said.

CHAPTER SEVEN

Home—and safe?

"Now, remember, Jessie," fussed Patrice. "You have to return the wings tomorrow morning, first thing. No matter what. They mustn't be out of the Realm for more than a day, or they'll begin to fade and spoil. All right?"

"I'll remember," promised Jessie. Clutching the precious wings, she bent and kissed Patrice on the cheek. "Thank you very much for breaking the rules for me," she said. "I hope you won't get into trouble."

Patrice beamed. "I don't see why I should," she said. "After all, no one knows about it except us."

"Jessie, Jessie!" The familiar trilling calls came closer as Jessie's five fairy helpers sped toward her. They landed, tumbling, in her hair. She laughed and tried to shake them loose.

"You aren't going home, are you?" asked Daffodil. "Not yet."

"Not yet, not yet," chanted the others.

"I have to," cried Jessie. "Now, be good and let me go!" She shook her head again, and Daisy and Bluebell fell bouncing and giggling onto the silken bundle in her arms.

Daisy sat up and looked at the soft mass of shimmering sky blue around her. "Wings!" she shouted in delight. "Jessie's still got her wings!"

"Jessie, will you dance with us again? Please, please?" All the fairies fluttered onto Jessie's fingers and began jumping up and down.

"Oh, shhh! Oh, please be quiet!" begged Jessie in alarm. She glanced at Patrice's horrified face. If the fairies went around spreading the word that she'd borrowed a pair of Queen Helena's wings, she and Patrice would both be in trouble!

Patrice stepped forward and raised her finger.

"It's a *secret* that Jessie is borrowing the wings," she said sternly. "You fairies aren't to say a word to anyone about it. Do you understand?"

The five fairies stared at her, wide-eyed.

"Don't say a word to anyone," Patrice repeated. "Or . . ." She hesitated, searching for a threat that was terrible enough to frighten them into keeping quiet. Then she had an inspiration. "Or Jessie will never be able to dance with you again!" she warned.

The fairies looked at one another. "We won't say anything. We promise!" said Daffodil. All the others nodded solemnly.

"Thank you," said Jessie, looking down at them.

"If we're good, and don't say anything, you *will* dance with us again one day, won't you?" murmured shy little Violet.

Jessie smiled. "Of course I will," she said.

She waved to Patrice and faced the hedge. "Open," she said. She closed her eyes. And then she felt the cool breeze stir her hair and brush her face as she disappeared through the black archway.

Jessie opened her eyes again in the secret garden. The wings were still clutched firmly under one arm. Her heart gave a great thump. She was home. She had the wings. Everything was going to be fine! She shook back her tangled hair and laughed as the tingling flecks of magic clinging there flew into the air.

She ran up to the house. The breakfast things were still on the table but she didn't stop to tidy up. She ran straight to her bedroom and went in, shutting the door behind her. Her butterfly costume—leotard, tights, and the headband that held the silver antennae—lay on the desk by the window. Spread out over them were the blue silk wings Granny had found in her storeroom.

Jessie unrolled the magic wings from the Realm and put them on her bed. She put the other wings beside them. They really did look alike, if you didn't examine them too closely. She didn't think anyone would notice the difference if she wore the Realm pair in the concert tonight.

They'd notice if she flew. But she wouldn't do

that, of course. The Realm wings would just make her graceful and lighter than air, as they had when she danced with the flower fairies. It wasn't really cheating, she told herself. Everyone would be happier if she danced well. Except maybe Irena Bins.

She folded the wings Granny had given her and hid them away on the top shelf of her cupboard. Then, carefully, she spread out the Realm wings on the desk in their place. She peered out the window. Gray clouds were gathering. Perhaps it was going to rain. She pulled the window shut, just in case. She didn't want the wings to get wet.

Feeling very happy, Jessie flung herself down on her bed. She yawned. She realized that she was very tired. No wonder—she'd had a busy morning. She yawned again, and decided to stay where she was for ten minutes. She'd just have a little rest. Mum and Granny wouldn't be home for an hour at least. She closed her eyes and put her hands behind her head. Just ten minutes. Then she'd go and tidy up the kitchen. Ten minutes . . .

But at the end of ten minutes, Jessie was sound asleep, her door and window tightly shut.

So she didn't hear the first sound—the scrabbling and scratching outside among the trees. And she didn't hear the second sound—the tiny voices desperately calling her from the secret garden. And she didn't hear the third, fourth and fifth sounds—Granny's big cat, Flynn, meowing from the kitchen, padding up the corridor toward her room, scratching at her door. Or even the sixth—the beating of the rain on the roof as it tumbled from the gray clouds at last, drenching the flowers and trees and streaming over the ground.

In fact, Jessie was sleeping so deeply that she didn't hear anything at all until Rosemary, her mother, opened her bedroom door an hour later and said, "Jessie, what are you doing sleeping at this hour? Aren't you feeling well?"

"What on earth's the matter with that cat?" Rosemary stared at Flynn, who was sitting by the back door, growling softly.

Flynn turned and blinked. Rosemary heaved two bags of groceries onto the cluttered kitchen table.

"Honestly, Jessie," she said. "I really wish you'd done what I asked and tidied the kitchen for when I came home." She reached over and crossly clapped the lid on the big brown sugar pot.

"Sorry, Mum," said Jessie, rubbing her eyes. She was still a bit dazed with sleep. She seized the sugar pot and took it to the pantry. Then she began to scuttle around putting the other breakfast things away.

Her mother started unpacking the groceries, glancing at her every now and then.

"Are you sure you're feeling all right, Jessie?" she asked, after a moment. "Are you nervous about the concert tonight?"

Jessie turned to her and smiled. "No," she said. "Not anymore."

Rosemary looked at her curiously. "Well, that's good," she said. "I'd started thinking that maybe you . . . oh well, never mind."

"Where's Granny?" Jessie asked.

"She's changing her clothes. She got wet at the shops, running around in the rain like a schoolkid." Rosemary shook her head and grinned. "We met the Bins from next door while we were dashing for the car. They looked at her as though she was crazy. She says it doesn't matter—they've always thought she was. Did you hear the rain, Jessie? It was a real spring storm. Sunshine one minute, heavy rain the next, then sun again. It's beautiful now."

She wandered over to the open kitchen door and looked out, her eyes dreamy. "So peaceful," she said. "So quiet and peaceful." Then her brow wrinkled. She leaned forward. Flynn backed away from the door and hissed.

Jessie's grandmother swept into the kitchen, wearing a long, soft blue dress. The charm bracelet on her arm jingled. Her thick white hair hung in a damp plait down her back. Her cheeks were pink and her green eyes twinkled. "What's Flynn complaining about now?" she laughed.

Rosemary turned around. "I think there's a big animal in the garden, Mum," she said. "Very big. I caught a glimpse of it just now, but then it disappeared behind the trees. Do the Bins have a dog?"

"No." Granny looked surprised.

Rosemary shrugged. "Oh well," she said. "Maybe it was just a shadow."

"Maybe," agreed Granny. But she frowned and went to the back door to look out herself.

A flicker of panic flared up in Jessie's mind. Just a flicker. But then she shook her head. No. There was nothing to worry about. The griffins were in the Realm, guarding the treasure house and Queen Helena's wings. And there was no way they could know that a pair of those wings was here in this house.

Was there?

At lunch, Granny was strangely silent. Flynn sat close to her chair, sometimes patting her ankle with his paw. Jessie's stomach felt upset and jumpy. Something was wrong. She could feel it.

As soon as they had finished clearing away, she ran up to her room again. She sat down on the bed, pressing her hand to her stomach.

"Jessie! Jessie!" A tiny voice sounded faintly in the stillness of the room.

Jessie sat bolt upright and looked wildly

around. But there was nothing to see. The only movement was the fluttering of a butterfly outside the window. She shook her head. She was hearing things. She took some deep breaths and tried to calm down.

"Jessie! Jessie! Jessie!" Now the voice was desperate. Jessie spun around. It was coming from outside!

She jumped up from the bed and ran to the window. A fragile, hovering splash of color danced behind the glass. The butterfly. Then Jessie narrowed her eyes. No!

Quickly she unlatched the windows and pushed them so they swung wide open. The tiny creature fluttered in and landed on her arm.

"Violet!" Jessie blinked at the trembling fairy in astonishment. "What are you doing here?"

"Oh, Jessie, Jessie!" panted Violet. Jessie bent down, straining to hear. It was hard enough to hear the fairy's voice in the Realm, but here it was almost impossible. And her body looked so small! No wonder humans sometimes couldn't tell the difference between fairies and butterflies. Jessie had made the same mistake herself.

"We . . . we came to warn you!" Violet clasped her hands. "The griffins!"

"What?" Jessie jumped. "What about the griffins?"

Violet burst into tears. "We were just talking—about you, and the wings." She sobbed. "You told us not to tell anyone, and we didn't. But we went to play in the red trees, near the treasure house, and we were just talking, and then . . . oh!" She put her face in her hands.

"The griffins heard you saying I had a pair of wings," said Jessie, trying to be calm. "Violet, is that what happened? Is it?"

"Ye-es," wailed Violet. "And the big one growled at the others, and one of them got up and flew off. And then we realized . . ."

"It's here, isn't it?" whispered Jessie. She remembered how Flynn had growled in the kitchen. She licked her lips. Her mouth was dry. "A griffin came through the Door to the Realm. It's looking for the wings."

Violet raised her head and nodded. Her tiny face

was pink and puffy with tears. "We followed it," she hiccuped. "Rose and Daffodil and Daisy and Bluebell and me. We saw it go out of the garden and up to the big trees around your house. We tried to call you, but you didn't hear us. And then . . ."

"Violet, listen," begged Jessie. "Where are the others? Calm down and tell me."

Violet swallowed. "It started to rain," she said. "And we got such a fright. We had to get under shelter, very quickly. That's the rule. Because if our wings get wet, we can't fly. And if we can't fly . . ." She swallowed again. "We panicked," she cried. "We did what they always say not to do. We all flew in different directions, looking for somewhere to hide. I got under a big leaf near the house. Then, when the rain stopped and I came out, I couldn't find the others. I called, and I looked, and I called. But . . ."

"You mean they're lost?" Jessie bit her lip. "You don't think the griffin could have . . . ?"

"Oh no. The griffin wouldn't hurt them," said Violet. "I don't even know where the griffin is, now. It flew off when it started raining. But Jessie, there are so many other dangers here! Cats, and spiderwebs, and deep holes and—and . . . Oh, where are they? Where are they?"

Jessie knew what she had to do. "Get onto my shoulder, Violet," she said. "And don't cry anymore. We're going to find them."

CHAPTER EIGHT

the search

Violet flew to Jessie's shoulder and crouched down among her long red hair. She was so light that Jessie couldn't feel her.

"Here we go, then," said Jessie, leaving the bedroom and shutting the door behind her.

Jessie could just hear the sound of Violet's tiny, panting breaths as she walked into the empty kitchen and toward the back door. She opened it and looked out. There was nothing to be seen but shadows moving on the ground among the tall, dripping trees. Shadows? Or . . .

"Where were you all standing when the rain

started, Violet?" she asked. "What could you see?"

"We were down there, near the entrance to your garden," said Violet's voice in her ear. "We could see through the trees, all the way up here to the house. The door was open. The griffin was coming up this way and we decided we'd have to follow it. Then the rain started. The griffin flew off, over to one side of the garden. The side near the fence." She waved a hand toward Irena Bins' house. "I think Daffodil went the same way, to keep an eye on it. Wait!" She paused. "Someone's calling!" Her voice was excited now.

Jessie listened hard. She couldn't hear anything.

"There it is again!" cried Violet. She tugged gently at Jessie's hair. "Jessie! I think it's Rose! I think she's here, in the house!"

"Rose?" Jessie looked around the tidy kitchen. "But where?"

"She's trapped!" squeaked Violet. "She can't get out. Oh . . . she says it's dark. She's frightened. Oh, Jessie help her!"

Jessie spun around, confused. *Think*, said a voice in her mind. *Don't panic. Think!*

208

Quickly Jessie went over what must have happened. The fairies had been looking up at the house from the secret garden. The back door had been open. Rose could easily have flown straight into the kitchen. No one would have seen her. Mum and Granny were out, and Jessie had been asleep in her bedroom.

Jessie clicked her tongue. If she'd cleaned up the breakfast things earlier, as her mother asked, she'd have seen Rose come in. She would have heard the story then. If only . . .

She gasped. The breakfast things. She had a flash of memory. Her mother, complaining about the mess, leaning over and banging the lid onto the big brown sugar pot. Rose was a plump little fairy. She probably loved sugar.

She rushed to the pantry, with Violet clinging to her hair. She pulled out the sugar pot and lifted the lid . . .

"Rose!" squealed Violet in delight.

Jessie scooped the pale, trembling pink figure from its prison and gently laid it in the palm of her hand. Violet fluttered down from her shoulder and the two fairies clung together.

"I thought you'd never come!" sobbed Rose. "Oh, I was just tasting a little bit of sugar. And then I heard voices, so I crouched down to hide. And then—then . . ." The sob became a wail. "I got locked in. And the lid was so heavy. I couldn't lift it! Oh, I thought you'd never find me! I thought . . ."

"Well, we did find you, Rose," soothed Jessie. "It's all right now." She sounded calmer than she felt. The brown sugar pot was only used in the mornings. Granny put sugar in her tea at break-fast, but the rest of the time she drank it without sugar, like Mum. If Rose hadn't been found, she would certainly have been trapped in the sugar pot all night. And there might not have been enough air in the pot to last that long. Even for a fairy.

Jessie shuddered. "We've got to find the oth-ers," she said urgently. "We've got to find them quickly."

She glanced at her watch. It was three o'clock. The concert began in two hours. There were still three fairies to find. And out in the garden the griffin was prowling. It wouldn't hurt the fairies. But Jessie, who had taken a pair of Queen Helena's precious wings, was another matter.

She looked out the back door again. Her feet felt heavy. She didn't want to leave the safety of Blue Moon, but she had no choice. She had a feeling that Daisy, Bluebell and Daffodil were in terrible danger. And she had to find them and help them, before it was too late.

"Get onto my shoulder," she said to Violet and Rose. "We're going outside."

Jessie padded through the wet grass along the side of the house, softly calling the fairies' names.

"I'm sure Bluebell and Daisy are together," Rose snuffled. "I'm sure they flew past me, heading this way."

Where could they be? Jessie peered into the flower beds, rubbed her eyes, peered again. But there was no sign of Daisy and Bluebell, or of Daffodil.

There was no sign of the griffin either. That

was one good thing, at least, thought Jessie. Though in a way she almost wished she *would* see it. Then at least she'd know where it was, instead of expecting it to leap out, screeching, from every bush and dark corner she passed.

"I flew all around the house," Violet piped up from her shoulder. "I called and called, as loudly as I could. But even though the rain had stopped, the water was running along the ground from the front and making a noise, so I suppose they couldn't hear me."

Jessie stopped. Violet was right. When it rained at Blue Moon the water did run down beside the house in streams.

"Hold on!" she said. Then she turned around and hurried back the way she'd come.

In the back garden the big trees still dripped. Jessie ran down among them.

"Jessie, they didn't come this way!" called Rose. But Jessie didn't stop. She knew exactly where she was going. She didn't think about the griffin, or the moving shadows to her right and left. She didn't think about anything except the danger she had suddenly understood.

The land on which Blue Moon was built sloped very slightly downwards, and when it rained water flowed from the front of the house to the back, trickling down into the trees. Jessie's feet splashed now as she ran on the soaked grass. She remembered finding quite deep puddles down at the bottom of the garden many hours after the rain had stopped. When she was little she used to sail leaves in them. Sometimes she would find drowned beetles, moths, butterflies . . .

"Help! Help! Help!"

The little voices were sharp with fear. Jessie's eyes widened, while on her shoulder Rose and Violet began calling and crying in answer.

"There!" shrieked Rose.

And then Jessie saw what Rose's keener eyes had seen before her. Clinging together, on a half-sinking leaf in the middle of a broad brown puddle, were Daisy and Bluebell. Their wings hung wet and useless down their backs. As Jessie watched, the leaf sank lower in the water. All the fairies screamed. Rose and Violet darted from her shoulder. They hovered helplessly over their friends, holding out their arms.

"I'm here," gasped Jessie, falling to her knees beside the puddle. She dipped her hand into the cold water and scooped up Daisy, Bluebell and the leaf in her palm. The two bedraggled fairies rolled off the leaf and lay still, panting, with their eyes closed.

"Take them into the sun!" cried Rose. Cupping the tiny bodies carefully, Jessie did as she was told, running out from among the trees and up to the back door where sunlight still warmed the stone steps. She sat down and opened her hand. The sun beamed down on the pale, wet figures lying there.

"Oh, poor Bluebell! Poor Daisy!" sobbed Violet, kneeling down beside them with Rose and stroking their faces. "Oh, their wings! Look at their wings!"

But Jessie could see that already the warm sun was doing its work. The sad, limp wings were beginning to dry. She sighed with relief. Bluebell and Daisy stirred and opened their eyes. After a moment they sat up. They spread out their wings and began opening and closing them gently.

"What happened?" asked Rose. "How did you fall into the puddle? You nearly drowned!"

"We . . . we made a terrible mistake," croaked Daisy. "We thought we'd be safe and dry close beside the house, under the eaves. And at first we were. Then, suddenly, all this water started running down, right where we were hiding."

"So we held onto the leaf." Bluebell shuddered. "But our wings got wet. And the water pushed us down beside the house, and over the grass, and down to that big puddle. We couldn't let go of the leaf or do anything. And we couldn't fly." Tears rolled down her cheeks.

"Don't cry, Bluebell," begged Violet. "Don't cry. Jessie found you. Just like she found Rose. You're safe."

Daisy sat up straighter. "But the griffin!" she exclaimed. "I'd forgotten. Oh, Jessie, did they tell you about the griffin?"

Violet and Rose nodded. "We don't know where it is," said Rose. Her lip quivered. "And

215

we don't know where . . ." Her voice trailed off.

Daisy stared at her for a moment. Then she twisted around, looking in all directions. "Daffodil!" she cried. "Where's Daffodil?"

CHAPTER NINE

Rescue

They wandered around the garden, calling in low voices, looking everywhere. Jessie trod carefully, her spine prickling, expecting every moment to hear the sound of the griffin. But they saw nothing.

"Daffodil flew that way, toward the fence," said Violet, pointing to the side of the garden. "I'm sure she did."

"We thought so too," chorused Bluebell and Daisy. They had quite recovered now, and were sitting high on Jessie's shoulder with their friends.

"But we've looked all along the fence," said

219

Jessie, glancing at her watch. She was terribly worried about bright, cheeky little Daffodil, and they were running out of time. Soon Mum would be calling her to go and dress for the concert.

"Let's look again. Please, Jessie!" begged Rose.

"Please, please, please," echoed the others.

Jessie sighed. "All right," she said. Again she trudged over to the side fence and began walking along it, looking in every direction and murmuring words of comfort to the fairies on her shoulder.

Suddenly she saw Mr. Bins, Irena's father, staring at her from the back steps of the house next door. Irena was with him, already dressed in her rainbow costume. Jessie wondered how long they'd been there, watching her. They probably wondered what she was doing. Maybe they'd seen her talking to the fairies. If they had, they probably thought she was talking to herself.

She saw Mr. Bins mutter something and Irena giggle, and felt herself beginning to blush with embarrassment. They already thought Granny was crazy. Now they thought she was too.

She turned her head away, and as she did so,

she saw Granny trudging up toward the house from the secret garden, Flynn at her heels. She couldn't see Jessie, hidden among the trees.

How odd, Jessie thought. I was sure Granny was inside. I didn't see her leave the house. She must have come out to the garden while I was around the front. Or even while I was in my room, talking to Violet. But what's she been doing down in the secret garden all this time?

For a moment Jessie thought of calling out to Granny and asking her to help. After all, Granny came from the Realm herself. And Jessie knew she had great powers. If anyone could find Daffodil, she could.

But as her grandmother came closer, Jessie realized she couldn't ask her. She was plodding rather than walking, looking neither right nor left. A fairy Queen she might be, but just now she looked small, frail, and terribly tired. She must have stayed out in the garden too long. After all, she had been ill and she was only just getting better.

Jessie walked on, trailing her hand along the

fence. A brown-and-orange speckled butterfly flew past her nose. Keep away from the Bins' house, butterfly, she warned it silently. You're a pretty one. Irena might decide she wants you for her picture frame.

Then she stopped and gasped aloud, gripping the fence so hard that her hand hurt.

"What's the matter?" cried the fairies on her shoulder. "Jessie! What's the matter?"

Jessie could hardly speak. Her teeth had started chattering with shock and fear. Suddenly she knew where Daffodil was. She knew it without a shadow of a doubt.

"I think . . ." she began. She swallowed, and began again. "I think the girl who lives next door might have mistaken Daffodil for a butterfly. I think she might have caught her, and taken her inside."

The fairies whispered together excitedly while Jessie pressed her lips together, trying not to panic. They didn't know what she knew about Irena and her butterflies. They didn't know that Daffodil was in terrible danger. They didn't know how hard it was going to be to save her—or that, even now, it might be too late. She peered through the fence. Irena would never let her just go in and take Daffodil. Even if she believed she was a fairy. *Especially* if she believed she was a fairy.

She made up her mind. There was no time to lose. "Wait here," she ordered. "Stay out of sight. I'm going to get Daffodil."

The fairies flew up into a tree and clustered together, holding one another's hands. "Good luck, Jessie," called Violet in a small voice.

Jessie crawled over the fence and crept up the path that ran along the side of the Bins' house. Several windows were open, but she didn't know where Irena's room was. She'd just have to get into the house and hope for the best.

She pulled herself up so that she could look into the first room she came to. It seemed to be a spare bedroom. Without really thinking what she was doing, she scrambled up and over the sill.

"Mum!" Irena's voice sounded piercingly just outside the room. Jessie's heart thudded. She scuttled over to hide herself behind the door.

"Mum, aren't you ready yet?" Irena demanded. "I want to go! I want to be early! I want to get there before that stupid Jessie does, or Ms. Hewson will be fussing over her as usual and won't have time to watch me practice my dance."

"All right, Irena, all right," called Mrs. Bins. Jessie heard her footsteps coming closer. "Dad's just getting the car. We've got plenty of time."

"Just come *on*!" snapped Irena's voice.

Jessie sighed with relief as the two sets of footsteps tapped away from the spare room and toward the back door. As it opened, Jessie heard her own mother's voice calling her.

"There, you see?" said Mrs. Bins. "Jessie's mother is only just calling her to get dressed. My goodness, they're cutting it fine, aren't they?"

Irena laughed unpleasantly. "Jessie's probably hiding," she sniggered. "Too scared to turn up at the concert. You'd feel the same if you danced like her."

The back door slammed shut. Jessie stood for a moment in the spare room, holding her breath. She was hot all over. What a horrible girl Irena Bins was!

She crept out into the short hallway that led to the front of the house. Irena's room must surely be up this way, she thought.

She was right. "Irena sleeps here," said the painted china notice on the white door next to the bathroom. Jessie pushed open the door and switched on the light.

There was the picture Sal had described. Irena in a beautiful butterfly costume, pink-and-silver wings outstretched. And all around the picture were butterflies, pinned to a board. Blue wings, orange-and-brown wings, blue-and-black wings. But, thank goodness, no bright yellow wings. Not yet. Jessie shuddered. Once she'd found a dead butterfly and taken it home. And once she'd seen a real butterfly collection in a museum. But how could *anyone* kill such beautiful things just to make a *picture frame*?

She spun around, searching desperately. And then her heart leaped. There, on a shelf, was a big jar. And fluttering weakly inside it, her tiny hands beating on the glass, was Daffodil. With a cry Jessie ran to the shelf, lifted down the jar and unscrewed the lid. "Daffodil," she breathed, tears springing into her eyes. "Oh, poor Daffodil."

She lowered her hand into the jar and Daffodil fell, exhausted, onto her fingers. Gently and carefully Jessie lifted her out. She could see that the little fairy was bruised all over.

"The human girl caught me in a net!" Daffodil cried. "After the rain. I could hardly breathe, in the jar. Oh, Jessie . . ."

"You're all right now, Daffodil," said Jessie grimly. She had never been so furious with anyone as she was with Irena Bins at the moment. "Come on. I'm taking you home." Holding Daffodil carefully, she ran to the window and began to climb out.

"The others . . . are the others all right?" called Daffodil. "And, Jessie, the griffin!"

"It's all right," soothed Jessie. "Everything's fine. Don't worry. Don't worry about anything."

She jumped down onto the path at the side of the house.

"Jessie! Jessie!" Mum was still calling. Jessie glanced at her watch again. Ten minutes to five!

And she wasn't even dressed. No wonder Mum sounded so desperate!

She raced down to the tree where the other fairies were waiting. They screamed with joy when they saw Daffodil, and flew to Jessie's shoulders like tiny birds. Still cradling Daffodil in her hand, Jessie ran for the secret garden.

She was late. She was terribly late. She was so late that Ms. Hewson would probably be very angry with her. She was so late that they might even start the concert without her, and let Irena dance in her place. And then Irena would be so triumphant! And Jessie would never have the chance to show her, and everyone else, just how well she could dance—if she had the right wings.

But it didn't matter. Nothing mattered except that all the fairies were alive and happy.

As she ran back up to the house to face her mother's worried, angry face, and then the crazy quick change in her bedroom and the terrible rush in the car to school, Jessie knew that she wouldn't have missed the chance of helping them for anything in the world.

CHAPTER TEN

The Butterfly

S al, golden in her sun costume, her spiky head-dress standing out all around her worried face, was hovering by the concert hall entrance as Jessie, Rosemary and Granny rushed from the car. "Jessie, where have you been?" she shouted. "Ms. Hewson's having fits!"

"I'm not surprised," snapped Rosemary. "Jessie, you've got mud on your face!" She dabbed at Jessie's cheeks with a tissue. "Goodness me, you're a mess! Couldn't you have cleaned yourself up a bit? No one asked you to change in the dark! Two seconds to turn on the light wouldn't have made a bit of difference."

Jessie didn't bother to answer. She just stood, panting, while her mother finished cleaning her face and quickly brushed her hair.

"Come on!" yelled Sal. "Everyone's on stage waiting!"

Jessie ran. "Good luck!" Rosemary shouted after her. Jessie raised her hand in reply, and the silk of her wings rustled. She smiled. She didn't need luck.

"Jessie!" shouted the class, as she and Sal came bursting through the side curtains and onto the stage.

"Shhh!" ordered Ms. Hewson. Her curly hair was practically standing on end. "Never do that to me again, Jessica!" she scolded. "I've aged ten years waiting here for you."

"She was trying to get out of coming, I'll bet," Irena Bins said loudly from the back of the stage. "I'll bet her mum made her."

"That's enough, Irena!" Ms. Hewson shot Irena a very unfriendly look. Then she looked at her watch. "It's time," she said. "Places, please. Good luck, everyone. And Jessie—just feel the music."

Jessie went behind the curtains at the side of the stage and waited. She heard the hum of talk from the audience in the concert hall die down as the lights were dimmed. She heard the music begin. She saw the curtains open. She saw Sal standing at the back of the stage, her arms outstretched. She saw the kids who were playing flowers swaying in time with the music. Soon the tune would swell and change, and then it would be her turn to go on. Mum and Granny would be watching her. All those hundreds of people would be watching her. Fear jabbed at her stomach.

She heard her music begin, and the old, awful, scared feeling turned her body to ice. Stiffly she raised her arms. Then she felt the silken blue wings float around her shoulders and down her back. At once the memories of her dance in the Realm came flooding back to her. The trees, the music, the golden air. Daffodil, Daisy, Bluebell, Rose and shy little Violet.

Jessie smiled. She ran onto the stage. Her wings

fluttered under the light. She swayed and turned. She was lighter than air. It was as if the music was part of her. She danced as she had danced with the fairies in the Realm. And she loved it.

Ms. Hewson watched from her place offstage. She tugged at her curly hair. She couldn't believe her eyes. But by the time the play was a quarter of the way through, her face was aching with smiling.

At the end, the audience clapped and cheered wildly. They clapped the sun, and the rainbow, and the flowers. They clapped the breeze, and the clouds, and the rabbits, and Ms. Hewson. But the longest claps, the loudest cheers, were for Jessie.

Jessie collapsed into the car, her head in a happy whirl of excitement.

"You were really marvelous, Jessie," said Rosemary, as they started home. "I had no idea you could dance like that. Had you, Mum?"

"I knew Jessie would be fine," said Granny mildly. "Once she learned to forget herself and just let the music lead her."

In the back seat, Jessie wriggled a bit uncomfortably. They wouldn't feel so proud of her if they knew about the borrowed wings.

Rosemary laughed. "I didn't think we'd make it," she said. "I really didn't. What on earth were you *doing* to make you so late, Jessie?"

Jessie shrugged in the darkness. "Mucking around," she said. "I, um, just ran out of time." That was true, anyway, she thought.

"Well, I must say you were very casual about the whole thing," said Rosemary. "I thought at least you'd have put out your costume ready to slip on."

Jessie sat forward. The car hummed along the road. "I did," she said.

Her mother shook her head. "Oh no you didn't," she said. "You'd started, but you'd forgotten the wings. When I went into your room, there were the leotard and tights and headband on the desk, and the window gaping wide open, and no wings! The wings were still in your cupboard. I had to get them out for you. They were up really high too. I nearly didn't see them."

Jessie's mouth fell open. Shocked, she peered closely at the blue silk wing dangling from her wrist. Her stomach turned over. She felt the edge of the silk with her fingers. Neat machine stitching. She gasped. These weren't the Realm wings. These were . . .

Granny gave a low, musical laugh. "Those wings looked pretty on you years ago, Rosemary, and tonight they looked just as pretty on Jessie," she said. "They've done good service."

Jessie slumped back against the car seat. She couldn't believe what she was hearing.

"I danced well," she said finally, in a small voice. "And I did it myself."

Rosemary laughed again. "So we've been telling you," she said. "Haven't you had enough praise for one night?"

"I think she's just realized what it all means," said Granny, smiling in the darkness and smothering a yawn.

Rosemary looked at her curiously. "And could I ask what you were doing this afternoon, Mum, to make you so terribly tired? You should take it easy, you know."

Granny inspected her charm bracelet. "As you

suspected, Rosemary, there was a rather large . . .
ah . . . creature in the garden. I decided it would
be best to send it home."

Jessie clapped her hand over her mouth to stop
herself from squealing.

Now it was Rosemary's turn to be surprised.
"Mum, why didn't you tell me?" she demanded.
"Jessie could have done that for you." She swung
the car into the Blue Moon driveway.

Granny shook her head. "Oh no," she said.
"Jessie had a few other little problems on her mind.
Five of them, I think. And the creature . . . knows
me. Besides, it had what it wanted from the house,
thanks to an open window. There was no point in it
remaining. I simply told it so, and—after a bit of an
argument—off it went." She turned around and
winked at Jessie.

"You mean some animal's been in the house?"
Rosemary exploded. She pulled the car up in front
of the garage and sat behind the steering wheel,
shaking her head. "What next! How can you take
these things so calmly, Mum?"

Granny opened the car door. Her charm

bracelet jingled on her wrist. "I take things as I find them," she said. "I move with the music, like Jessie. I find that's always the best way."

Jessie couldn't wait to get inside the house. She had to think. She ran to her room to change, her head spinning. The griffin had stolen back the magic wings from her room while she was helping the fairies. Granny and Flynn had sent the griffin home, and it had taken the wings with it. Mum had put out the old wings, and Jessie had hurriedly put them on in the dimness of her room without noticing the difference. She had danced in wings that were no more magic than her black leotard. And Granny had known, all the time.

Jessie went to her window. Mum had left it slightly open so that the soft evening breeze came through. Soon the moon would be rising. And Daffodil, Rose, Daisy, Bluebell and Violet were safe at home again.

"Goodnight, little fairies," Jessie said. Then she saw something lying on the desk just beside the window. A small scrap of gold silk tied with silver thread. There was something hard inside. She unrolled the silk carefully. A golden butterfly slid into her hand. Another Realm charm for her bracelet. And there was a note. *Thank you, Jessie,* the note read. *We'll always remember.*

Jessie sat down and fixed the golden butterfly to her bracelet, beside the heart that already hung there.

She looked out the window again. "And thank you," she whispered.

The bracelet tinkled as she took off her blue silk wings and slipped the silver headband from her hair. The concert was over and so was this amazing day. But in her mind Jessie could still hear music. She could still hear the fairies laughing, the screeching of the griffin, Patrice's chatter, Giff's wails and bossy Maybelle giving orders. She could still see the ring of tall trees, the golden air, the cloud of fairies dancing against the blue sky, the shimmering wings spread out on a yellow silk bedcover. She could still feel the tiny weight of the flower fairies on her shoulder. The glorious feeling of flying.

She looked at the bracelet again. The fairies were right. They would always remember today, and so would she. This had been the kind of day that no one could *ever* forget.

Fairy Realm

BOOK 3

The third wish

CONTENTS

wishes

"I wish I could go to the pool today," sighed Jessie, looking out the Blue Moon kitchen window at the fierce blue sky.

Her mother didn't answer, so Jessie tried again, raising her voice over the sound of the early morning news droning from the radio.

"It's going to be really hot again today," she said. "I *wish* you didn't have to go to work, Mum. Then you could take me swimming."

She looked sideways at her mother. But Rosemary still didn't answer. She didn't even seem to be listening. She switched off the radio and started rushing around with a piece of toast in one hand and her car keys in the other, the belt of her nurses' uniform dangling behind her.

Jessie edged toward her. "I wish it wasn't so *hot*," she complained. "I didn't think it *ever* got as hot as this in the Mountains. I wish we were somewhere cooler. I wish Granny's car was fixed so *she* could take me to the pool. I wish—"

"I wish I could find my sunglasses!" snapped Rosemary. "And I wish you'd stop complaining and being so selfish, Jessie! Think what other people are going through. These terrible fires . . ." She bit her lip and turned away.

Jessie went back to the window and frowned at the sky. There wasn't a cloud to be seen. Just haze from the smoke of burning bushland. And the sun, rising higher, beating down on the house, making everything hot, hot, *hot*.

The clock ticked in the silence of the kitchen.

"At least you don't have to go to school in this heat, Jess," Rosemary said more brightly. "Think yourself lucky you're on holidays."

"Some holiday," grumbled Jessie. "Everyone

else will be at the pool today, while I'll be stuck here, bored and boiling and—"

"Jessie, that's *enough*!" Rosemary exploded.

Jessie jumped, then stuck out her bottom lip and sulked. Her mother hardly ever shouted at her, and she didn't like it.

Granny came into the room with her big ginger cat, Flynn, at her heels. She was frowning, and her green eyes looked worried.

"I met Hazel Bright on my walk," she said. "She says that another big fire broke out early this morning—just outside Silvervale."

"So I just heard on the news," Rosemary answered, as she struggled to fasten her belt. "They're fighting it with everything they've got. But people are starting to panic. It's panic that's the real killer, you know. People forget to think when they panic."

She shook her head. "It's going to be a bad day. It's so dry, Mum. Everything's so dry. And this heat—and the wind . . ."

"Dreadful," nodded Granny. "If only it would rain." She sighed. Flynn twined around her legs.

Rosemary shrugged. "If only," she said. "But wishing won't make it happen, will it?"

She found her sunglasses behind the teapot, put them on, and hurriedly ate the last of her toast. "Well, I'm late," she said. "I'll have to go." She looked seriously at Granny. "Now, Mum, ring me if you're worried about anything, won't you?" she murmured. "I don't like leaving you and Jessie here without the car."

"Don't worry, dear," Granny said. "I know what to do. All will be well."

"I hope so." Rosemary picked up her handbag. "You be good for Granny, now, Jessie," she warned. "Do everything she says. And no more carrying on about the pool. Go and paddle in the fish pond or something."

"*Yes*, Mum," said Jessie. She hunched her shoulders and turned away to look out the window again. "I wish *I* was a fish," she muttered.

She heard her mother click her tongue crossly, but didn't look around.

Granny didn't say anything until Rosemary had gone. Then she walked over to Jessie, her eyes twinkling, and tickled the back of her neck. The charm bracelet on her wrist jingled like tiny bells.

"Don't be crabby, Jessie," she teased.

"Mum's the crabby one," said Jessie shortly. "She's been crabby for days."

"She's hot, she's tired and she's worried about the fires," Granny said. "At the hospital they're treating lots of people who've been injured trying to save their homes. It must be very hard for Rosemary—for all the doctors and nurses. Most of them are probably worried about their own houses and families too."

"Mum doesn't have to worry about *that*, though, does she?" Jessie demanded. "So . . ."

She broke off as she caught sight of Granny's grave face.

"She's *not* worried about it, is she?" she squeaked. "I mean, there's no danger *Blue Moon* could get burned, is there?"

Flynn meowed loudly. Granny bent to stroke his head. "Nothing's safe in this part of the Mountains at the moment, Jessie," she said gently.

"Not even Blue Moon."

Jessie stared at her, open-mouthed. She could hardly take it in. It seemed impossible that the old home she loved so much could be in danger.

"The fires are moving closer to us all the time," Granny went on. "Didn't you hear what we said about Silvervale? That's not far from here at all. And they're fighting to save houses there right now."

Jessie's heart thudded. "I didn't think," she whispered. "I didn't know. Why didn't Mum tell me before?"

"Rosemary didn't want you to be frightened," said Granny calmly. "But I think it's time you understood how things are. You and I both know that you can be very brave if you try. The charms on your bracelet are proof of that."

Jessie glanced at the charm bracelet on her wrist, took a deep breath, and nodded.

Her life had changed in more ways than one since she and Rosemary had come to live with Granny at Blue Moon. Because right at the beginning Jessie had discovered her grandmother's secret—the invisible Door at the bottom of the garden that led to the fairy world where Granny had been born. The world called the Realm.

In the Realm Jessie had had some amazing adventures. And at the end of each of them she'd been given a charm by the Realm Folk, so she'd never forget.

Forget? she thought now, looking at the charms one by one. As if she could ever forget the Realm, or the wonderful, exciting times she had had there. But, she remembered, there had been some hard and dangerous times too. Often she'd had to be brave. Braver than she'd ever thought she could be.

Even so, the idea that her beloved Blue Moon might burn down was very frightening indeed.

It must be frightening to her mother too, she realized. Now she understood why Rosemary, usually so calm and cheerful, had been scratchy and impatient over the last couple of days. And imagine how Granny must feel!

She looked at her grandmother, whose eyes were thoughtful as she scratched Flynn's upturned chin. Blue Moon had been her home ever since she had left the Realm as a young princess, to marry the human man she loved.

Jessie clasped her hands tightly. "Granny," she said. "Can't *you* do something about the fires?"

"If that were possible, I'd have done it long ago, Jessie," Granny said. "I still have some powers, that's true. But it takes very, very powerful magic to change the weather."

"Could Queen Helena do it, then?" Jessie asked. "I could go and ask her." She jumped up, filled with excitement. "Yes! Queen Helena is your sister. She'd want to help. I could . . ."

But Granny was shaking her head. "Helena can't help us either, Jessie," she said. "In the mortal world her magic is no stronger than mine."

But Jessie wasn't going to give up so easily. "Well, isn't there anyone else?" she cried. "Surely there must be *someone* in the Realm whose magic will work here strongly enough. Someone—or something . . ."

She broke off. Granny's face had grown suddenly thoughtful.

"What is it?" Jessie exclaimed, clapping her hands.

Granny touched her charm bracelet with long, slim fingers. "Something," she murmured. "Yes, of course. How could I have forgotten?" She frowned. "It's been so long since I've even thought about them, you see."

"*What?*" Jessie begged.

"Well," Granny said slowly, "when you said 'something,' I suddenly remembered. About wish-stones."

a warning

"What are wish-stones?" Jessie asked eagerly. "Do they make wishes come true? What do they look like?"

"Come with me," Granny said. She walked briskly from the kitchen, and Jessie followed.

Granny led the way to the studio where her husband Robert, Jessie's grandfather, had painted the fantasy pictures that had made him famous.

Everyone thought that Robert Belairs had just imagined those scenes of fairy Folk, gnomes, elves, mermaids and miniature horses he painted so beautifully. Jessie used to think so too. But now she knew better.

Grandpa had painted things he had actually seen, in the Realm. Long ago, he, like Jessie, had discovered the Door to the fairy world. And, like her, he had visited it often.

The visits had stopped, of course, the day he and Granny had run away to get married. He couldn't go back after that. Granny's parents had been angry with him, and with their daughter. A fairy princess marrying a human man? Giving up her right to rule as true Queen? That was unheard of in the Realm.

But Granny had never been sorry about the choice she had made. In time her parents had forgiven her. And she was very happy at Blue Moon. Though she was now the Realm's true Queen, her kind sister Helena ruled in her place. And Granny lived on in the mortal world that was now her home.

Robert Belairs was dead now, but his paintings of the Realm had been printed in books and hung in art galleries all over the world. Many of them were on the walls at Blue Moon too. Jessie loved them.

Every painting seemed to sparkle with magic.

Jessie looked around the studio. It still smelled and looked the same as it had when Grandpa was alive. Everything was just as he'd left it.

Granny crossed the room to a small desk in one corner. She picked something up and held it out for Jessie to see.

"There you are, Jessie," she said. "A wish-stone."

"But that's just the stone Grandpa used to hold down his papers," Jessie cried in disappointment.

She'd seen it often, when she'd come to the studio to watch Grandpa paint. She'd held it in her hand and played with it, many times. It was that kind of stone. Smooth, rounded and a speckly-gray color, it fitted into your hand as though it liked to be there. But there was nothing magic about it. Nothing at all.

Granny stroked the stone. "Robert kept it because it reminded him of the Realm," she said. "But it's empty. The wishes are gone."

"Gone?" Jessie didn't understand.

"Every wish-stone can grant three wishes,"

Granny explained. "Once the wishes have been used up, the stone is—just a stone. It looks the same, but it has no magic power any more. Like a battery that's dead."

"But how can you tell?" Jessie asked. "I mean, are you *sure* this one is empty?"

Granny nodded. "Oh yes. You can tell by the way it feels. Anyone from the Realm can tell a live wish-stone from an empty one. Live ones make your fingers tingle."

Jessie licked her lips nervously. "Would *I* be able to tell?" she said.

"Probably," said Granny cheerfully. "After all, you *are* my granddaughter." Then, as Jessie's eyes lit up, she shook her head.

"But we can't depend on a wish-stone to stop the fires, Jessie," she said. "You can't just go to the Realm and find one, if that's what you're thinking." She put the wish-stone back on Robert's desk and walked to the studio door.

"Why not?" asked Jessie, running after her.

"Because wish-stones are very rare," Granny answered. She began leading Jessie down the hall and back to the kitchen. "They're found in Under-Sea, the mermaids' domain. Realm Folk only find them when they are washed up on the shore of the Bay. Realm Folk don't visit Under-Sea."

"Grandpa did," Jessie said, pointing at one of her favorite paintings. It had hung on the wall at the end of the Blue Moon hallway for as long as she could remember.

The painting showed mermaids and mermen swimming in a garden of light green seaweed and palest pink coral. Brightly colored fish flitted through the coral like birds. Tiny, fairy-like creatures with pretty silver fins instead of wings rode seahorses over soft white sand.

In the center of the picture two handsome merpeople sat on a smooth rock, playing with a small mermaid child with light brown hair. A young mermaid with shining black hair stood nearby. Behind them, the crystal spires of palaces shone through transparent blue water.

Granny turned to look at the painting. "Yes," she agreed. "Robert often went to Under-Sea. Being human, he was always welcome in the merpeople's palaces. Realm Folk are not. It is the Rule."

"Granny, I'm a human," Jessie exclaimed. "Or mostly. So I can go to Under-Sea and bring back a wish-stone!"

Granny stared at her. "I suppose you could try," she began slowly. "But . . ." She hesitated.

Jessie jumped up and down impatiently. "What, Granny?"

"If you *do* find a wish-stone, you must be very, very careful, Jessie. Wish-stones can be very dangerous."

"How?"

"They are very powerful," Granny said. "In all the Realm there is only one wish-granter more powerful. Whoever holds a wish-stone can wish for almost anything, and that wish will come true. But the wish is forever. You can't take it back."

"But that's wonderful, isn't it?" Jessie couldn't see the problem.

"It's wonderful," Granny agreed. "But surely you can see that it's very dangerous too, Jessie? Just think of all the wishes you've made this morning."

Jessie shook her head in bewilderment. The wishes she'd made this morning? What was wrong with them?

"Think about it," Granny urged.

Jessie thought. She'd wished she could go to the pool. She'd wished her mother didn't have to go to work. She'd wished Granny's car was fixed. She'd wished it wasn't so hot.

But then, with Granny's eyes looking gravely into her own, Jessie remembered another wish she'd made. She'd wished she was a fish.

She thought about what might have happened if she'd been holding a wish-stone in her hand when she made that wish, and she felt sick.

Granny nodded. She could see from Jessie's face that she'd finally understood.

"So you see, Jessie," she said gravely, "sometimes we all make wishes that we don't really mean. And of course that doesn't matter at all, usually. But with a wish-stone it does matter. It matters a lot."

"Yes, I see." Jessie swallowed. "I'll be careful, Granny," she promised. "I really will. If I find a wish-stone I won't make any silly wishes. I won't even *think* them."

"Well, see that you don't." Granny tried to smile. "How would I explain it to Rosemary if she came home to find you had fins and a tail?"

She patted Jessie's shoulder. "All right," she said. "If you're going, you'd better get ready as quickly as you can. There's no time to lose."

CHAPTER THREE

TO the palace

J essie and Granny walked down from the house, through the trees, to the tall hedge that surrounded the place they called the secret garden. The grass was crisp and dry under their feet, and a scorching wind tossed the branches above them.

Jessie was wearing only a light sundress, with her swimsuit underneath, but she felt very hot all the same. Hot—and frightened.

She followed Granny through the opening in the hedge and stood with her on the smooth grass in the center of the secret garden. She breathed in the tangy scent of rosemary rising from the bushes clustered around the edge of the lawn.

Usually Jessie felt peaceful as soon as she entered the secret garden. It was as though the tall hedge kept the whole world out. But today the smell of smoke mingled with the scent of rosemary. Today the air was filled with fear.

"Now," Granny said. "The first thing you must do is go to the palace. You'll need help to get to the Bay."

Jessie nodded. Her friend, Patrice, was the housekeeper at the palace. Patrice was always glad to see her. And perhaps Maybelle, the bossy miniature horse, and Giff the elf would be there too. They would help her. She knew they would.

"Be back by afternoon-tea time," Granny warned. "No later." She looked up at the hazy sky. "The fires are getting closer," she murmured.

She spun round to face Jessie. "All right," she said. "Go! Go quickly!"

She held up her hand. "Open!" she commanded.

Jessie heard the familiar rushing sound as the Door began to open. She closed her eyes and felt the cool breeze surround her, lifting her long red hair off her shoulders and blowing it around her head.

Then suddenly she remembered something.

"Granny," she called. "If the wish-stones are the second most powerful wish-granters in the Realm, what's the first?"

With the sound of the opening Door filling her ears and her mind, she struggled to hear Granny's answer. It could be important. If she couldn't find a wish-stone, maybe she could dare to go to the most powerful wish-granter of all to get the fires stopped.

But when Granny's answer came, sounding small and far away, she was very surprised.

"Magic fish," Granny called.

Fish? Had Granny really said "fish"?

Jessie strained her ears to hear over the rising and falling of the wind. "Magic fish," cried Granny's voice. "But don't . . . magic fish . . . rules . . . Under-Sea . . . no use . . ."

Then her voice disappeared completely, and Jessie was whirling away.

Into the Realm.

❋ ❋ ❋

265

Jessie opened her eyes and blinked in the golden light. She had arrived.

The pebbly road was solid under her feet. Behind her, the magic hedge that protected the Realm from invaders stood green and glossy.

Everything looked beautiful and peaceful as always. The sky was a soft, clear blue. The trees by the roadway whispered gently to each other.

And there, nibbling grass under the shade of one of the trees, was a tiny white horse.

"Maybelle!" Jessie called out in delight.

The little horse lifted her head. The red ribbons in her mane fluttered in the breeze. Jessie ran to hug her.

"Well, well, well!" exclaimed Maybelle. "Where did you spring from?"

"I've come because I need help," Jessie said. "I need to find a wish-stone."

Maybelle snorted. "Oh, is that all? No problem!"

Jessie's mouth fell open. "No problem?"

"Oh no!" Maybelle pawed the ground. "Any-thing else you'd like, while we're at it? The ten crowns of Lillalong? The golden horn of the uni-corn? The giant pearl of silence? A sensible brain for Giff the elf?"

Jessie smiled to hide her disappointment. "Oh, you're teasing me," she said.

"Just a bit," said Maybelle. She tossed her mane and showed her teeth in a horse laugh. Then, catching sight of Jessie's face, she stopped laughing.

"Something's wrong," she said.

"Yes," sighed Jessie. "Maybelle, I really, *really* need to find a wish-stone. Blue Moon's in danger. And not only Blue Moon. There are terrible bush-fires in the Mountains. The fire-fighters can't stop them. We need rain. We need it now! You've got to help me!"

Maybelle frowned. "I'll do what I can. But find-ing wish-stones isn't easy, you know," she warned.

"I know," said Jessie. "Granny told me. But I'm going to Under-Sea to try."

Maybelle snorted with shock. "Under-Sea?" she repeated. "Queen Jessica said you could go *there*?" She paused. "Listen, I think you'd better go and see Patrice about this," she said. "She'll know what's best to do."

She trotted off toward the road with Jessie following.

"What if Patrice isn't home?" Jessie worried, as they began walking toward the palace.

"Oh, she is," said Maybelle. "Or she *was*, half an hour ago. I was there myself, but I had to leave. Giff was with her. I had to get away from him before he drove me crazy. He's being sillier than usual today, and that's saying something."

Jessie giggled. She couldn't help it. She might be excited, and worried, and even a little bit scared. But the thought of Giff always made her laugh.

The great front doors of Queen Helena's golden palace were standing wide open, but Maybelle and Jessie slipped around to the little side door that led to Patrice's own apartment.

Jessie knocked.

In a moment she heard footsteps, and then the door was opened.

"Jessie!" cried Patrice. She held out her arms,

and her black button eyes shone. "How lovely to see you! Giff's just gone to the palace kitchen on an errand for me, but he'll be back soon."

"Worse luck," growled Maybelle, nudging Jessie forward with her nose. "Now listen, Patrice. You and I have a big problem to solve. Jessie wants us to help her find—wait for it—a wish-stone!"

She nodded solemnly at Patrice, who was staring at Jessie in surprise.

"That's right," Maybelle went on. "A wish-stone. Jessie needs it. Badly. I've told her wish-stones are impossible to find. But she—"

"I don't know about impossible," Patrice called back over her shoulder, as she led them down the narrow corridor to her kitchen.

"Is that right?" snorted Maybelle. "I suppose you can tell us just where one is, then, can you?"

They went into Patrice's cozy kitchen, and Jessie sat down at the table in her usual place.

Patrice bustled to the cupboard. "As a matter of fact, Maybelle," she said, pulling down a cookie tin from the top shelf, "I can."

Maybelle sniffed. "Go on, then," she jeered. "If you're so smart!"

Patrice smiled. And from the cookie tin she pulled a round, gray-speckled wish-stone!

CHAPTER FOUR

Giff Gets into Trouble

Jessie sprang to her feet. Her chair crashed to the floor behind her. "Patrice!" she yelled. "You've got one! You've got a wish-stone!"

Maybelle shook her head at the stone lying on the table. She nuzzled it with her nose and jumped back. "It's a live one too."

"Of course it is," said Patrice.

"But where did you get it?" demanded Maybelle.

Patrice shrugged her plump shoulders. She looked a bit embarrassed. "I took a splinter out of a griffin's wing a couple of weeks ago, and the next day it brought me the stone. It must have had it for years and years."

"Humph!" Maybelle pawed the floor. "Pretty good thank-you present."

"Yes," Patrice admitted. "I tried to give it back but the griffin wouldn't take it. You know how they are. It's not full, you know. By the feel of it, it's only got one wish left in it. Anyway, I was saving that for a special occasion. And it looks as if this is it."

"You mean I can *have* this stone?" cried Jessie. She couldn't believe her luck.

"Of course you can, dearie," said Patrice warmly. "After all you've done for the Realm, it's the least I can do. Now, sit down again and tell me what's been going on." She put a jug of cool-looking pink drink on the table, and went back to the cupboard to get out another cookie jar.

"Well, this *is* handy," said Maybelle, watching Jessie rescue her fallen chair and draw it up to the table. "Now you won't have to go to Under-Sea, Jessie. And a good thing too."

Patrice, coming back with a plate of honey

274

snaps, looked shocked. "I should think so!" she exclaimed.

"But why shouldn't I have gone?" Jessie asked. Of course she was very happy to have found a wish-stone so quickly and easily, but in her heart she was rather sorry that now she didn't have an excuse to visit the mermaids.

"It's *much* too dangerous." Patrice shook her head. "*Much*!"

"Granny didn't think so," protested Jessie.

Patrice looked puzzled. "How *could* Queen Jessica be happy for Jessie to go to Under-Sea? With Lorca sitting in the Bay on that horrible Island, just waiting to—"

"Who—" Jessie began.

"I know why," Maybelle broke in. "It's because Lorca and the Island only appeared about fifty years ago. You remember, Patrice. At the blue moon. The time of the renewal of the magic."

"Oh, of *course*," sighed Patrice. "And Jessica left the Realm at around the same time, with Robert. So she never heard about Lorca. She thinks Under-Sea is still as safe as it used to be."

"Who's Lorca?" asked Jessie, getting her question in at last.

Patrice shuddered. "Better not to know, dearie," she said. "You won't have to worry about her now, anyway. You've got your stone. You've got your wish. Have a cookie."

"Cookie?" squeaked a voice from the door.

"Here's trouble," growled Maybelle.

Giff the elf came tiptoeing into the room. He squealed when he saw Jessie, and ran to sit down beside her, his big pointed ears waggling with excitement.

Jessie was delighted to see him.

Maybelle was not so pleased. "For goodness' sake, sit still, Giff," she humphed. "Don't talk, don't wriggle, don't do anything."

"Can I have a cookie?" Giff asked in a small voice.

Patrice laughed as she poured the drinks. "I suppose so," she said. "But just one. You've already had three this morning."

Giff helped himself, beaming. He wriggled closer to Jessie. "Honey snaps are my favorite," he whispered to her.

He swallowed the last crumb and his eyes darted back to the plate. His fingers crept across the table.

Maybelle made a disgusted sound, then bent to drink.

"No more honey snaps, Giff," warned Patrice, turning away to refill the jug.

"I wasn't!" protested Giff, looking guilty. His fingers swerved from the cookie plate to the stone lying beside it. "I was just looking at this."

He picked up the stone. "But it's not fair," he whimpered, playing with it while he looked longingly at the plate. "I *adore* honey snaps."

"Ah, Giff," murmured Jessie. "I don't think you'd better—"

Maybelle's head jerked up sharply.

"I could eat a million of them," sighed Giff.

"Giff!" shouted Maybelle. "Put that—"

"I wish I *had* a million of them, all to myself, right now."

There was a cracking sound and a puff of smoke.

Giff screamed. And then Jessie was screaming too. Because suddenly she couldn't move. She couldn't see. She was buried in a mountain. A mountain made of a million honey snap cookies.

It took a long time for them to get out of Patrice's kitchen. The honey snaps were piled as high as the ceiling and had blocked the door. But finally, mainly thanks to Maybelle's strong hoofs, they were all standing out in the air, brushing themselves down.

"What's happened?" Giff wailed. "Why do these things always happen to me?"

"Because you're a meddling, idiotic elf who can't keep his hands to himself, that's why!" roared Maybelle, stamping her feet. Cookie crumbs sprayed from her mane in a honey-smelling shower.

Patrice was furious too. "That was a *wish-stone*

you were playing with, Giff. A *wish-stone!*" she raged. "And now you've used up the last wish. You . . . you . . ."

"I didn't know!" squealed poor Giff. "I didn't know! It's not my fault!"

"Whose fault is it then?" hissed Maybelle. "Jessie *needed* that wish. She needed it badly. And now it's gone."

Giff began to sob as though his heart was broken. His ears drooped miserably.

Jessie put her arms around him. "Giff, it's all right," she said. "I know it was an accident. Don't cry." She bit her lip. She was terribly upset and disappointed. But she couldn't bear to see Giff so sad.

"I'll just go to Under-Sea, as I'd planned," she went on. "I'll find another wish-stone."

Giff sobbed even more loudly. "To Under-Sea?" he wept. "But, Jessie, if you go there Lorca might get you, like she got that young mermaid, long ago. And all those other creatures since. Oh no! And it will be all my fault!"

"Jessie," Patrice exclaimed. "You absolutely can *not* go to—"

"I have to go!" Jessie insisted. "There's no way out of it now."

Giff groaned and buried his face in his hands.

Maybelle was slowly shaking her head.

"Please, Maybelle," Jessie begged. "Please. You've got to show me the way to Under-Sea."

Maybelle shut her eyes and went on shaking her head. "No, no, no!"

Jessie stuck out her chin stubbornly. "Well, if you won't show me the way, Maybelle, I'll just find someone else who will!" she said.

Maybelle opened her eyes and looked deep into Jessie's own. Then she sighed. "All right," she said. "If you're determined to do this, I suppose I can't stop you. I'll take you as far as the Bay. But after that you'll be on your own, Jessie. I can't go with you to Under-Sea. None of us can."

Jessie's stomach gave a nasty little lurch. But she knew she had no choice. If Blue Moon was going to be saved, she had to find a wish-stone.

And if Under-Sea was where wish-stones were found, Under-Sea was where she had to try, whatever the danger.

Maybelle tossed her head. "Well, if we're going, let's go." She began trotting down the pathway beside the palace.

Giff's lips trembled. He clutched at Jessie's skirt. "I'm coming too," he said.

"Well, I'm staying," said Patrice grimly. "To clean a million honey snaps out of my kitchen. Though how I'll ever do it I don't know."

She thought for a moment, then she nodded. "I'll get the Palace Guards to come and help me with it," she said. "They all love honey snaps. They'll eat the kitchen clean in no time."

"Good!" said Jessie. She hugged the little housekeeper goodbye. "Now, don't worry about me, Patrice," she said. "And thank you for offering me your wish."

"Take great care, Jessie," Patrice whispered. "Come back to us safely."

With a final wave, Jessie and Giff scuttled after

Maybelle, down the narrow path.

"Where does this lead?" Jessie asked.

"To the river," wailed Giff. "To the wet, cold, scary, watery, awful river!"

CHAPTER FIVE

The River

G iff was still sniffling when they reached the river. Jessie sighed. She wished he wouldn't. Crying wasn't going to help. And besides, though she was feeling scared at the thought of the adventure ahead of her, she couldn't help feeling rather excited too.

The river was beautiful. Through its sparkling pale blue water, where tiny silver fish darted, you could see a bed of smooth white pebbles. Grass and flowers grew thickly along its banks, and it wound away into the distance like a ribbon laid out on a green carpet.

Maybelle trotted to the water's edge and stood there peering back toward a bend in the stream.

"What's Maybelle looking for?" Jessie asked Giff, hoping to take his mind off his troubles.

"A river-float," sniffed Giff. He blew his nose on a large green-and-white-spotted handkerchief. "One should be coming along any time now. Just be ready to jump in when it arrives. Those awful flying fish don't like to wait. They're *so* impatient."

Flying fish?

Jessie was just about to ask some more questions when she heard a strange sound. A whistling, splashing sound.

"At last!" snorted Maybelle.

Jessie looked up, and caught her first glimpse of a Realm river-float. It rounded the river bend and came speeding toward them, dazzling in the sun. Whatever she'd been expecting, it was nothing like this!

Six great silver fish, with rainbow fins spread wide, leaped together like dolphins through the pale blue water. Behind them, pulled by silver ribbons and skimming on a froth of white bubbles, raced a curved float that gleamed like glass.

The whistling sound grew louder. The river water began lapping up onto the grass. Jessie's heart thudded with excitement.

"Hold up your hands!" ordered Maybelle. "Get ready!"

The flying fish saw the waving hands and steered for shore. While their passengers piled into the rocking float, they tossed their heads impatiently. Water sprayed from their rainbow fins and scattered in sparkling drops from the silver ribbons.

"Hold on tight," Maybelle warned the others. She settled herself in the front of the float, behind the fish. "Ready?"

At the back of the float, Giff whimpered and clung to Jessie. The craft heaved and dipped in the water. Jessie held tightly to the smooth, glassy edge and grabbed Giff's coat with her free hand. She didn't want him to fall overboard.

The fish made a clicking noise and swished their tails. Jessie could tell that they were anxious to be on their way.

"To the Bay!" called Maybelle, nudging at the silver ribbons. And with a mighty leap the fish were off, the float speeding behind them.

Within moments they had reached full speed and had begun to sing their strange, whistling song again. And then the float started to skim over the surface of the water like a hovercraft. It was almost flying on a carpet of bubbles. Jessie gasped with delight as the wind beat into her face.

"Isn't this *wonderful*!" she squealed to Giff beside her.

Giff moaned softly. His eyes were tightly closed and he was looking very pale. Jessie hoped he wouldn't be sick.

They flew along, leaving a trail of white froth behind them. On each side the green banks slipped away. Every now and then Jessie saw a village surrounded by fields of pink flowers and golden grass, or a group of miniature horses grazing, or elf children hanging from the trees, waving and calling. Sometimes there were green-haired water sprites too, staring silently at them from their secret homes behind the reeds that grew at the river's edge.

Jessie lost all track of time. She stared till her eyes were sore as the countryside flashed by. She didn't want to miss anything.

"Won't be long now," called Maybelle. "The Bay is up ahead."

Over the backs of the flashing, leaping fish, Jessie saw the broad blue waters of the Bay, ringed with rocks and white sand. She shook her head in amazement. How could they have reached it so quickly? It seemed to her that they had been traveling for only a few minutes. Had they been going so fast?

Maybelle saw her surprise. "Time goes fast on the river, Jessie," she shouted over the whistling of the flying fish.

"Not fast enough for me," whispered Giff.

The float began to slow down. The fish swerved toward the bank.

"This is as far as they go," called Maybelle. "From here we walk down to the Bay. Then I'll call an Under-Sea guide for you."

Before Jessie could ask her what she meant,

the float had swept around on its ribbons and bumped gently into the bank. The fish began making their clicking noises and thrashing their tails.

"Out!" ordered Maybelle.

Jessie and Giff scrambled out onto a neat square of sand covered with white pebbles like the ones on the riverbed. Jessie stumbled and almost fell. Her knees felt wobbly and her head swam.

She realized that whatever she had thought, they really must have been on the river for quite a long time. It had been early morning when they started off, but now the sun was much higher in the perfect blue sky. No wonder her legs felt strange, walking on dry land after hours cramped up on the speeding float.

She sniffed the salty, sea-smelling air and blinked at the countryside around her: low bushes studded with small purple flowers, blue-green grass poking through sandy ground.

Maybelle clambered from the float, the ribbons in her mane fluttering in the breeze. She turned and dipped her head to the silver fish.

"Thank you," she called.

The fish raised and lowered their rainbow fins in reply. And then they leaped away from the bank, turned, and sped back the way they had come, the empty float skimming behind them. Their whistling song floated back to Jessie as they disappeared into the distance, leaving a trail of white behind them. Soon they were out of sight, and only the splashing of the water on the riverbank showed where they had passed.

Following Maybelle, and holding Giff by the hand, Jessie climbed up from the riverbank to a low hill and looked out over the Bay.

It was calm and still. Water rippled gently against the white sand of the beach. Beyond the Bay Jessie could see the deeper blue of the open sea, stretching away into the distance. But guarding the entrance to the sea, right in the middle of the gap, was the dark, jagged shape of a rocky island. It looked like a blot on a pretty picture — out of place and ugly.

Jessie felt Giff's hand tighten on hers and she shivered. She felt very far away from home now. Very far away from the palace and the Door that led to the secret garden at Blue Moon. She thought of the fires. Of Granny waiting for her and trusting her. Would she be able to find a wish-stone before it was too late?

"Once upon a time you could have found a wish-stone anywhere along there, if you looked long and hard enough," Maybelle said, nodding at the white shore of the Bay. "They used to get washed up on the sand once in a while. But now . . ."

"What happened?" Jessie asked.

"Some Folk say that when Lorca's Island came up out of the sea, it changed the way the tide worked," Giff said. "They say that's why the wish-stones aren't washed up here any more."

"The Island came up out of the sea?" exclaimed Jessie. "Just like that?"

Maybelle nodded, frowning at the ugly Island. "Lorca's magic must be very powerful," she said. "One day the Bay was clear. The next, the Island was sitting there, right at the entrance. Blocking the way to the open sea."

"You could swim around it," Jessie pointed out. "Or sail."

"You could," Maybelle agreed. "And the fish and mermaids and other creatures do move in and out, of course. They have to, to gather food. But they keep well away from the Island. If creatures swim too close, or the tide sweeps them too near its shores, they are drawn into it. And no one ever sees them again."

Jessie stared at her in horror. "But how awful!" she cried. "Why doesn't Queen Helena stop it?"

Maybelle flicked her mane. "Queen Helena does not interfere with the workings of Under-Sea," she said. "The creatures of Under-Sea love her as their Queen, but rule their own domain. That is the Rule."

Jessie shook her head. "Who is this Lorca? Where did she come from?"

"No one knows," said Giff. "She just . . . appeared one day, at the time of the blue moon."

"We didn't take much notice at first," Maybelle added. "Just then no one cared much about anything except the news that Princess Jessica had left the Realm. But then we heard that a young mermaid had been taken. And now everyone fears the

Island. You must keep well away from it, Jessie."

Jessie nodded. "Of *course*, Maybelle," she said. The idea of going anywhere near that black rock in the Bay scared her to death. She wasn't going to fall into the evil Lorca's clutches. No way.

ʀɪρρle

Maybelle made her way down the narrow, overgrown path that led to the Bay. Jessie followed. The purple-flowered bushes tickled her bare legs as she walked, and the sand was warm under her feet. She could hear Giff stumbling along behind her.

Soon the three friends were standing on the soft white sand. Strange shells and pieces of seaweed lay in heaps along the shore. Crystal-clear water lapped gently at their feet. Giff squeaked and jumped back as it reached for his toes.

Near to where they were standing was a huge

bell, like an old-fashioned school bell, hanging low to the ground. It looked as though it hadn't been used for a very long time. Salt crusted its golden surface, and grass had grown up around the short wooden posts on which it hung. Maybelle plodded over to it.

"All right, then," she said, shaking her mane. "Are you ready?"

Suddenly Jessie didn't feel ready for anything. "What do I do?" she whispered.

"You don't do anything," said Maybelle. "You just stand and wait."

She turned her back on the bell and kicked out with her back legs, striking it with her tiny hoofs once, twice, three times.

A low ringing sound filled Jessie's head. She put her hands over her ears, but still she could feel the ringing through her fingers. She saw the waters of the Bay start to shimmer. Small caps of foam appeared here and there.

"Oh, stop it, stop it!" squealed Giff, wrapping his arms around his head.

Maybelle bared her teeth. The sound was

hurting her ears too, but she scanned the water in silence, watching carefully for any sign that her message had been heard.

Slowly the ringing died away. Jessie took her hands from her ears.

"Nothing's happening at all," she exclaimed in disappointment.

"Wait," murmured Maybelle. "Stand still and wait."

Jessie did as she was told. The small waves rippled over her toes. The warm sun beat on her back and shoulders.

"There," said Maybelle at last. "There!"

Jessie squinted at the shining water. At first she couldn't see anything. And then she drew a sharp breath of excitement. A groove in the surface was moving swiftly toward them. It was as if something was swimming deep down, very fast.

She rubbed at her eyes and stared again at the water. A shape was rising slowly up out of the depths.

The shape came closer and closer. And then, suddenly, a head crowned with a mass of floating light-brown hair broke through the surface. A sweet, pale face was smiling at her. And then there were white shoulders and arms, and the glistening silver of a tail.

A mermaid!

Jessie swallowed. She didn't know what to do or say.

Maybelle stepped forward and nudged at her, pushing her further into the water.

"This human child wishes entrance to Under-Sea," she said. "Will you guide her?"

The mermaid bowed her head. She lifted her hands from the water and threw something. Jessie caught it. It was a necklace, made of shells and pink coral.

"Put it on," said Maybelle.

"Do I have to?" whispered Jessie. The necklace looked pretty but it was hard and prickly, and she was sure it would be uncomfortable to wear.

"Yes," Maybelle told her. "You'll need it. Unless you can breathe better under the water than most humans can. And be quick, Jessie. She won't wait for you long."

Jessie understood. She pulled off her sundress so that she was just wearing her swimsuit. She threw the dress onto the sand. Then she slipped the necklace over her head. The mermaid watched her with large, unblinking blue eyes.

Maybelle shook her head. "I don't like this," she said. "I wish I could go with you."

"I'll be all right, Maybelle," Jessie answered firmly. But she sounded much braver than she felt. Only the thought of Blue Moon made her step forward. She started wading out into the water, toward the mermaid. The water reached her waist . . . her chest . . . her shoulders . . .

"We'll wait for you, Jessie," Giff called. "However long it takes, we'll be here."

Jessie turned back to see that he had picked up her dress and was clutching it in his arms. He was trying to be brave, but tears were rolling down his cheeks. Maybelle was looking straight ahead, her eyes dark with fear, her mane whipping in the wind.

Jessie stood on tiptoe and lifted her arm to wave. Cool fingers, soft as velvet, grasped her other hand. She looked around. The mermaid was beside her, smiling. A smooth tail brushed against her legs.

And then the fingers were pulling her out of her depth, and the water was closing over her head. And she was being drawn down, down, away from the land and the air and the sunlight. Into Under-Sea.

Jessie was seized with panic. Everything had happened too quickly.

She struggled desperately against the mermaid's grip, but the cool fingers, so soft to touch, were strong. She couldn't get away. Her eyes were shut tight, her head was spinning. She felt as though her lungs were bursting.

"Breathe, little human, breathe, or you will die." The voice rippled and sighed in her head. It was like nothing she had ever heard before. She forced her eyes to open.

The mermaid was facing her, her own beautiful blue eyes wide. Her tail moved gently in the water.

Her hair floated around her face and shoulders like a cloud.

"Breathe!" There was the voice again. But the mermaid hadn't moved her lips.

Then Jessie realized that the sound was in her mind. The mermaid was speaking to her without using her voice. She was so surprised that she gasped. Bubbles of air escaped from her mouth and lungs.

"Breathe!" insisted the gentle voice.

Jessie did. She knew she had no choice. And the moment she began, she knew that the magic of the necklace had worked. She could breathe just as easily in this clear salty water as she could on land.

She almost laughed with relief.

The mermaid smiled and let go of her hand. "My name is Ripple," her voice whispered in Jessie's mind. "Now, follow."

With a flick of her tail she began to swim through the clear blue water. Down, down, down.

Jessie swam after her. She swam more easily than she ever had in her own world. Her long red hair streamed behind her as she cut through the cool water like a fish. She had never felt so at home in the sea.

As they swam deeper, the light grew dimmer, until everything was blues and greens. Long strands of seaweed trailed across their path. Tiny fish circled them.

"Where are we going?" Jessie tried to call. But her voice was lost in the water. Ripple swam on.

Jessie tried again. But this time she remembered where she was. She didn't say the words aloud. This time she *thought* them, as hard as she could.

Ripple slowed, then drifted around to face her. "We are going to the crystal palaces," Jessie felt her say. "Is that not what you wish?"

"I . . ." Jessie didn't quite know how to answer. She didn't know exactly where she needed to go. All she knew was that she had to find a wish-stone as quickly as possible. Time was running out.

"Time . . . wish-stone?" said Ripple.

Jessie jumped. But then she realized that of course the mermaid could hear what she was thinking. She nodded. "I am here to find a wish-stone."

Ripple pressed her hands together. Jessie could feel her worry and sadness.

"The stones you seek come from far away, in the deep Under-Sea, outside the Bay," she said. "And for long and long, they have not come into our waters. The tides still bring them in from outside, but they do not reach us. They are all drawn in—to the Island."

Jessie felt a stab of terrible disappointment. "Oh no!" she exclaimed.

Ripple clutched her hands to her chest. Jessie's pain had hurt her as if it were her own.

"Ripple, what's the matter?"

A small gold-colored fish swam up to them and started nosing the mermaid anxiously. He had felt her distress too.

He looked crossly at Jessie. "What have you been doing to Ripple?" he thought at her, in a piping, bubbly voice.

Jessie shook her head. "Nothing!" she said. "I just felt—sad."

"Well, don't!" piped the fish. "Keep your human thoughts to yourself. Don't go round hurting others with them. *If* you don't mind."

He left Ripple and moved closer to Jessie. He was a very funny-looking fish, she thought. His golden body was small and round, and his tail and fins were very big and flappy. He had wide, poppy eyes and a bossy sort of expression.

"Don't be so rude!" he snapped. "You're not so good-looking yourself. Look at those legs. Two of them! And not a fin to be seen. Yuck!"

Oh dear, thought Jessie. I'll really have to learn not to think so loudly down here.

"Yes, you will," said the fish, as though she'd spoken aloud. Then he looked at her suspiciously. "And anyway, how did you find your way here? No human has been to Under-Sea for many long years."

Jessie lifted her chin. "My Realm friends brought me," she answered proudly. "I am Jessie, the granddaughter of Queen Jessica and Robert Belairs."

CHAPTER SEVEN

what to do?

T he little fish's big eyes popped. "Seaweed
and thunder!" he gasped. "Robert's grand-
child!" He swam round and round her, staring.

"Did you know my grandfather?" Jessie asked.

"*Know* him? Of course I did," the fish said. "I
was his guide times without number, in Under-
Sea. I showed him things no other human has ever
seen. The coral gardens. The crystal palaces. The
Living Wall. Ah . . . we had great times together."

"We all loved Robert, in Under-Sea," said
Ripple, gliding up to join them. "We were very sorry
that he couldn't come back to see us any more."

"My fins we were," sighed the fish. He turned to Jessie. "And now his granddaughter is here," he said. "Come to see the sights. Well, I'll be glad to show them to you."

"Jessie hasn't come to see the sights," Ripple told him. "She's come to try to find a wish-stone."

The fish flicked his tail. "You know there's no chance of that," he said. "Lorca's grabbed every one that's come into the Bay for the last fifty years."

Jessie felt desperate. "Will you guide me to the Island, then?" she demanded. She knew she shouldn't even think of it. She knew what Patrice and Maybelle and Giff would say if they knew. But what else could she do?

"We cannot do that," Ripple's voice breathed in her mind. "We cannot go near the Island."

"But I need a wish-stone so *badly*," cried Jessie. "My home—Queen Jessica's home—is in danger. Only a wish-stone can help me save it!"

"Look, I think you should come with us to the crystal palaces," said the little fish. "We'll discuss the matter there."

He darted away in a flash of gold. Ripple

smiled at Jessie through her floating, billowing hair. "Follow," she sang, beckoning. "Follow."

Jessie followed.

Arriving at the place Ripple and the golden fish called "the crystal palaces" was exactly like walking into the Robert Belairs painting hanging in the hallway at Blue Moon.

There were the gardens of seaweed and coral, the fish flitting around like birds, the merpeople gliding through the blue water. And there were the palaces themselves, their crystal spires shining blue and silver.

Mermaids and mermen clustered around Jessie and Ripple, smiling and sending messages of greeting.

All of them had the same bright, unblinking blue eyes, but their hair was of many different colors — from light brown, like Ripple's, to black, dark brown, blue-gray, soft yellow, white and even pale green. Their tails were all different too. Some were silver, some were gold, some were spotted or striped with blue, green or purple.

The tiny-finned fairy creatures that Jessie had seen in her grandfather's Under-Sea painting were there too. They laughed and dived around her head, sometimes riding on their seahorses, sometimes leaping off and swinging on her floating hair.

"They love your hair," Ripple's voice laughed in Jessie's mind. "No one in Under-Sea has hair the color of the sunset."

Jessie was pleased. Her hair had never been described in such a lovely way before.

Ripple took her by the hand and led her a little away from the crowd to where two older merpeople were sitting together on a smooth rock.

As she came closer to them, Jessie realized that she had seen them before, sitting on that same rock. They were the merpeople her grandfather had painted playing with their child.

"Jessie, please greet Aqua and Storm, my mother and father," said Ripple, bowing her head.

Jessie jumped. Her mother and father? Then Ripple must have been the brown-haired child in the picture. Of course, many years had passed since it was painted. Ripple had grown up. She looked around for the other mermaid in the group, the one with shining black hair. Jessie knew that she would not look very different. In the Realm, people didn't age as they did in the mortal world.

"Mother and Father, please greet Jessie, granddaughter of Queen Jessica and Robert Belairs," Ripple was saying.

Warm feelings flowed to Jessie from Aqua and Storm as they smiled at her. They were strong and beautiful-looking. Aqua's silver hair was like a floating curtain that fell almost to the tip of her tail. Storm's hair was long too, but it was bound back with a string of plaited grass.

"We are pleased to greet you, Jessie." Aqua's rich voice said. "It is long and long since we saw a human here. And your grandfather was our dear friend. He often shared a meal with us."

"Mother and Father," Ripple said softly, "Jessie has come to us for help. Her home is in danger. She needs to find a wish-stone."

Aqua and Storm looked at one another, and Jessie caught some of the thoughts that passed between them. Wish-stone — Island — Lorca. Then a terrible, aching sadness. And a picture of a young mermaid with shining black hair.

Jessie looked at Ripple and felt a sadness in her too. She hesitated, confused and worried.

"They're thinking of their lost daughter."

Jessie spun around to see the little golden fish at her ear.

"Lost?" she whispered.

"Coral, Ripple's older sister, was lost long and long ago," he told her. "The first of many creatures lost to Under-Sea since the Island came."

"Lorca took Ripple's *sister*?" cried Jessie. She looked in horror at Aqua and Storm, and at Ripple. Their wide, unblinking blue eyes stared back at her, filled with pain.

She remembered Giff and Maybelle talking about a young mermaid who had disappeared. This must have been Coral.

"She is a prisoner on the Island," whispered Ripple. "Still, after all these years. Sometimes, at night, we hear her singing. Sad, sad and far away."

Jessie was filled with anger. "Why don't you try to get her back?" she cried.

"We tried, when we first realized what had happened." Aqua's voice was despairing. "We used every wish-stone left in Under-Sea to try to break Lorca's power. But it was no use."

"Then you should go to the Island yourselves," Jessie urged, "and *force* Lorca to give Coral up!"

They shook their heads. "We cannot breathe the air," they said together. "We cannot walk the land. Lorca is safe from us, on her Island."

"Then ask Queen Helena to help you!" Jessie exclaimed. "She could send her guards, in a boat. They could . . ."

But again they were shaking their heads. "The sea and the land are separate in the Realm," they said together. "The Folk cannot help us. That is the Rule."

Jessie frowned crossly. She was starting to get very impatient with the Rule.

"Lorca has captured many creatures," Storm said. "But Coral was the first. And the only mermaid to be taken. Now we are too careful to fall into Lorca's net. We keep away from the Island."

"The fish aren't too careful, though," the golden fish's piping, bubbling voice chimed in. "The young ones are easy prey for Lorca. Sometimes they escape her nets to tell the tale. That's how we know her name and what she does. But often they don't escape. And then they are lost."

"Coral was young and foolish too," sighed Aqua. "But so filled with life. Oh, how she loved to listen to Robert's stories of the mortal world, Storm. Seeing his granddaughter makes me remember."

Again a feeling of sadness swept over the little group.

"We are sorry," Storm said, putting his arm around Aqua's shoulders. "We would give you anything we had for Robert's sake, Jessie. But sadly a wish-stone is not in our power to grant."

"Once they were everywhere in Under-Sea," said Aqua. "Our Coral had them by the ten and twelve."

"I remember," Ripple put in. "I was only little, but I remember Coral's wish-stones. She carried them with her always, in a net made of her own hair. They were her treasures."

"Coral loved the wishing," said Aqua. "She loved new things. Different things. It hurts me to remember that we argued about it, the last time we saw each other. She said she was bored, stuck here in this quiet Bay. I was angry with her. It was the time of the blue moon. There was much to do."

Jessie looked up. Just like Mum and me this morning, she thought. How strange. I guess children and parents are the same, wherever they live.

"She swam away from me, angrily, toward the deep ocean," Aqua went on sadly. "I did not worry at first. I thought she would come back safely, as she had before. But I had not counted on Lorca. That very day the Island rose from the seabed. And I never saw Coral again." She put her face in her hands.

Storm touched her shoulder and bowed his head.

Jessie felt Ripple speaking to her. "Come away, Jessie. We need to talk."

"Ripple? I heard that! What are you planning?" piped the little golden fish, swimming after them as they glided away.

Ripple lifted her small, pointed chin and looked at him. There was a determined expression in her strange blue eyes. "Come with us and see," she said. "You might even be able to help. After all, you must have some uses, magic fish."

CHAPTER EIGHT

The Dark Shadow

"What did you call him?" Jessie tugged at Ripple's hand, making her stop and listen. "Magic fish? Why did you call him that?"

The little fish waggled his big tail importantly. "Because that's what I am!" he said.

"But—but Granny said you were really powerful," Jessie stammered. "And I was imagining you'd be . . . well, you know—bigger."

"Well!" huffed the fish. "Good things come in small packages, you know."

Suddenly, like a bolt of lightning, Jessie realized what all this meant. She didn't need to find a wish-stone any more. She'd found something much, much better.

"Oh," she screamed. "Then if you're the magic fish, you can grant my wish, can't you? You can save Blue Moon!"

The fish blew bubbles and shook his head. "Sadly, I'm no use to you," he said. "As I am no use to Aqua and Storm. Don't you think they would have used me to get Coral back, if they could? I can only grant wishes to people who catch me by accident, and then let me go again. That's the Rule."

The Rule again!

"That's crazy," Jessie shouted. "Crazy!"

The fish waved his fins. "I can't help that," he said. "It's always been the Rule. I'm surprised Queen Jessica didn't tell you about it."

Jessie stared at him. "Actually, she did," she admitted. "Or she tried to."

"*No use . . .*" Granny had called, trying to make her voice heard over the rushing of the Door. "*Magic fish . . . rules . . .*" She'd been trying to tell Jessie that the magic fish couldn't help her, because of the Rule.

"Why can you only grant wishes when you're caught by *accident*?" Jessie asked in despair.

"Think about it," said the fish scornfully. "How could I live otherwise? Everyone wants a wish now and then. If they could get three of them just by catching me whenever they felt like it, I'd never be out of a net! My life would be a misery."

"Yes, I can see that," whispered Jessie. She felt close to tears. Oh, I just don't know what to do, she thought. Soon I'll have to go home again. And I'm still no closer to finding a wish than I've ever been.

"Listen," said Ripple. "I've been thinking. I think you should try to get onto the Island."

"Well, I think so too!" exclaimed Jessie. "But I'll never find the way on my own. And you said—"

"That was before," Ripple said grimly.

"Before what?" Jessie asked.

"Before I realized something—just now, when we were talking to my mother and father. The Rule forbids us from asking Realm Folk to help in our domain. But you're *not* of the Realm, Jessie. You're human." She paused.

"Oh no," mumbled the magic fish. "Ripple, no!"

But Ripple ignored him. "So I'll lead you to the Island, Jessie, on one condition. When we get there, you can find your wish-stone. But then — you have to help me get Coral back!"

"You're crazy, Ripple!" The magic fish was so upset that he started swimming in circles. "You can't risk going to the Island. And you can't let Jessie risk it either."

Jessie and Ripple faced him and linked arms.

"We're going," Ripple said. "And that's that."

Jessie nodded.

"I'll tell your mother and father," warned the fish.

"No you will not," snapped Ripple. "Or I'll never speak to you again! Don't you realize that Jessie is our only chance to save Coral, magic fish?"

She stared at him with fierce blue eyes.

He waved his fins helplessly.

"Don't you want Coral home with us again?" Ripple went on. "Don't you want my mother and father to be happy?"

"Of course I do," the little fish said. He sighed and blew a bubble. "All right. I'll help you. But I don't like it. I don't like it at all."

Jessie didn't have any idea where she was. She just swam after Ripple and the magic fish wherever they led. They brushed their way through trailing seaweed branches, following some sort of trail that only they could see.

The water was rougher now. It was also sandy and full of tiny bubbles. It was hard to see very far ahead. So it was a shock to Jessie when suddenly she felt Ripple's fear.

"What is it, what is it?" she called, swimming forward as fast as she could.

"The Island is very close," Ripple's voice sighed in her head. "See . . . there . . ."

Jessie squinted through the cloudy water and saw a dark shadow rising up in front of them.

"What will we do now?" she asked.

"Swim away as fast as we can, if you ask me," grumbled the magic fish.

"No!" sang Ripple. "Jessie, you must go to the surface. Climb up the rocks onto the Island. Try to find out where Coral is being kept prisoner. Then come back and tell us, so we can make a plan."

"I don't need to come back," Jessie objected. "We can talk with our minds."

"No we can't. This way of talking does not work between land and sea," Ripple told her. "Once you are on land we will not be able to hear your thoughts, and you will not be able to hear ours."

They had stopped swimming, but they were still moving closer and closer to the dark shadow ahead. And they were moving fast.

"The tide is strong," warned the magic fish, beating his fins against the current. "It's pulling us in to the Island, Ripple. Much too quickly. We had better —"

His words broke off with a shout of fear.

Jessie's head echoed with the shock of it, and with Ripple's terror and her own. Because suddenly they were tumbling toward each other, crashing together, knocking heads and bodies helplessly.

Jessie felt Ripple's tail lashing against her legs. She felt the magic fish, hopelessly tangled in her streaming red hair, struggling to free himself.

Then they were being dragged along—not just by the current, but by something else, something they could feel but couldn't see.

"A net!" Ripple cried. "We're caught in a net!"

"Help me!" bubbled the magic fish. "Help me!"

With all her strength, Jessie tore against the web that had trapped them. But it was terribly strong. As it pushed against her face, she saw it— a fine black net that was almost invisible in the dark, cloudy water.

Panic swept over her. She started beating against the net, thinking of nothing except escape, feeling the others struggling in the same way, knowing it was hopeless.

And then, crystal clear in her mind, came the

memory of her mother's voice; familiar, ordinary, full of human common sense. *"Panic is the real killer,"* Rosemary had said in the kitchen this morning. *"When people panic, they forget to think."*

Even in a magic world, that was true. Jessie knew she had to think. Stop struggling helplessly. Stop screaming and crying for help that couldn't come. Think!

She grabbed the panic-stricken Ripple with one hand. She put her arm around her and held her close. At least that way they wouldn't crash against one another. "Be still," she thought. "Be still!"

As she felt Ripple quieten she put her other hand behind her head and pulled at her hair, untangling it so the magic fish could swim free. His bubbling cries stopped as her fingers did their work. He darted, gasping, over her shoulder and took shelter between her and Ripple.

Then, clinging together, they let the net pull them in.

The dark shadow grew closer and closer.

"We're going to crash into the rocks!" thought

Jessie, and panic nearly seized her again. But then she saw that there was a patch in the shadow that was even darker than the rest.

It was a cave. And they were being dragged toward it!

"The Island is hollow," Jessie told the others. "We're being pulled inside it. Hold on!"

Then with a rush they were plunging into blackness. They heard the whisper of something closing behind them, sealing the cave, trapping them inside.

Ripple screamed. Jessie shut her eyes tightly. The magic fish shuddered against her chest.

And then they were spinning and going up. Above them, someone was hauling them in.

The spinning rush upward stopped. The net that held Jessie, Ripple and the magic fish hung swinging in the water.

Jessie opened her eyes. She was dizzy and weak. Just above her, she could see the surface. And there was light, but it wasn't sunlight.

Without warning, the net that held her tangled with Ripple and the magic fish dropped away. Jessie didn't realize what had happened at first.

Then she understood.

They no longer needed to be held in the net because they were in an underground lake. The cave that was the entrance to the lake had been sealed with a door of some kind. Now they were trapped—inside the Island.

Other creatures were in the lake too. Although she couldn't see them, Jessie could feel their thoughts. Maybe they were hiding—or maybe they were being held in some other part of the lake.

"Coral! Coral! Are you here?" Ripple had felt the other creatures too. She was calling her sister.

But there was no answer.

"She isn't here," said the magic fish. "Lorca must be keeping her in some other place."

"How do we know she's on the Island at all?" asked Jessie.

"We know," said the fish grimly. "That net—the net that caught us—was made of her hair."

Jessie felt sick.

Ripple clung to her, shivering with fear. Jessie put her arm around her shoulders. What was going to happen now?

"Come to me!" thundered a voice from above them. "Come to me!"

CHAPTER NINE

Escape

Holding Ripple and the magic fish, Jessie let herself drift slowly upward. She knew there was no point in hiding. There was no way out of this trap.

Her head broke through the surface of the lake. She looked around. They were in the center of a huge cave. Darkness gloomed at its sides and in its rocky ceiling, but around the lake hundreds of candles burned. Their flickering light lit up the water's surface and played on the speckled gray wish-stones that lay heaped around the lake's shore.

But Jessie barely glanced at the wish-stones. All her attention was fixed on the figure that stared down at them from a rocky platform. A woman with flowing hair and gown, her face in deep shadow. She was leaning forward, searching the water to see what she had caught.

"I am Lorca, little fish!" cried the woman. "Welcome!" Her voice echoed from the rocky walls of the cave.

"We are not fish," called Jessie. "Lorca! Let us go!"

The woman jumped back as if someone had hit her.

"What?" she cried. "Mermaids? Oh no! No! What have I done?" She fell to her knees and buried her face in her hands.

Jessie and Ripple looked at one another. This was not what they had expected.

The magic fish wriggled out of Jessie's grasp and stuck its golden head out of the water.

"Let us go, Lorca!" he piped angrily, thrashing his tail. "Let us go, and all the other creatures you have taken."

Lorca's head jerked up. She gasped. "Can this be true?" her booming voice echoed. "Have I caught you, magic fish? At last?"

"What do you mean, at last?" bubbled the magic fish.

"I have been casting my nets for you, all these long years." The voice was like the beating of a drum. "I have waited so long. Now I have you! At last! I have you—and I will set you free. And so I claim my wishes."

"If you have been fishing for me, you cannot claim your wishes," bubbled the magic fish. "By the Rule, I must be caught by accident."

"No!" Lorca's shout was deafening. "No! This is the only way! The only way! I have tried the wish-stones. I have gathered a hundred of them, but they do nothing. Nothing!"

Jessie pulled at the magic fish's tail and made him put his head below the surface again so that they could speak in secret.

"For goodness' sake, fish, don't tell her you can't

grant the wishes," she told him fiercely. "If she thinks she can have what she wants, she'll let us go!"

"We cannot go without Coral," Ripple insisted. "If we get away, we must take her with us. You must ask for that, magic fish. You must . . ."

"I cannot lie," said the fish. "It is the Rule."

"Fish, our lives are at stake! Forget the Rule for once," Jessie exploded. "And anyway, even if Lorca *has* been fishing for you for years, she didn't know when or if she'd catch you, did she? So this *was* an accident, in a way. How do you know the magic won't work for her?"

"What if it does? It may be worse than if it does not," murmured Ripple, her thoughts filled with fear. "Because what will Lorca wish for? Something so great that even a hundred wish-stones cannot do it. It could be something of great evil."

"She could wish to spread her power over the whole of Under-Sea," suggested the fish with a shudder.

"Why would she want to do that?" asked

Jessie. "What use could she make of the power? She's a land person, like me. She breathes air and has no fins or tail. She can't . . ." She broke off. She put her head above the surface again and looked at Lorca. A wild idea had come into her mind.

Her thoughts began to race, tumbling over each other. Yes. Yes, it could be . . .

But what if she was wrong? She was tired, and weak from the struggles in the net. Did she dare to risk facing that frightening figure on the rocky platform? Letting her know that she was not a mermaid at all, but human?

Well, she had to try. All their lives depended on it. And so did Blue Moon. Even now Granny must be wondering where she was. Even now the fire must be getting closer, closer . . . She began swimming quietly to the edge of the lake.

"What are you going to do?" Ripple called after her in terror. "Are you still trying to get a wish-stone? Jessie, don't get out of the water! She cannot get to you in here. Out there, she can—"

"Don't worry, Ripple," Jessie called back. "Just wait. If I'm right . . ."

Slowly she pulled herself onto the rocky shore.

Her legs trembled as she climbed toward the shadowy figure standing above her. She had been a long time under the sea, and she had grown used to swimming instead of walking.

A shriek echoed from the rocky platform.

"A human! But . . . ?"

Jessie shivered with cold and fear. She forced her shaking legs to take the last few steps. The woman in the shadows drew breath sharply as she came closer.

"Stay back, human child," cried Lorca. "Are you not afraid? Do you not know who I am?"

Jessie looked her full in the face. She was beautiful. Her long black hair fell like a curtain around her slim shoulders. Her white feet were small and bare. Her blue eyes were filled with terrible sorrow.

"Yes, I do," Jessie answered. She heard her own voice echoing against the rocks. It sounded deep and strange. "I know who you are and I know what you've done," she said, staring straight into the sad blue eyes. "Once, long ago, you took wish-stones and wished. You wished for what you have now. And then you found you didn't want it after all. But the wish couldn't be undone."

The figure before her groaned.

"I know who you are and I know what your name is," Jessie went on softly. "Now you call yourself Lorca. But years ago, in Under-Sea, your name was Coral."

There was a scream from the lake. It was Ripple. She had heard everything. "Coral," she was sobbing. "Coral! Sister!"

"Ripple," breathed Lorca. She began to clamber down the rocks, scratching and bruising her feet and legs. She threw herself down by the edge of the lake, reaching out.

Ripple held up her arms. Lorca went toward her. Her hair fell over her shoulders like a heavy black veil. "Ripple, my little sister. I did not know you. I did not know . . ."

"My grandfather, Robert Belairs, told you stories about the human world, didn't he?" Jessie said.

"Yes," whispered Lorca. "I thought he could take me there. My mother and I had an argument. I ran away. I was so angry." She gave a shuddering sigh. "I took all my wish-stones and made my wishes," she said. "I wished I could breathe air and walk on land. I wished for an island near the mouth of the Bay, where I could wait for Robert. I didn't think. I didn't remember the wish-stone Rule. I had never wished for anything important before."

The magic fish made a sad, bubbling sound.

"I wished for a new name," Lorca went on. "A name made of the same letters as my own, but different, and not like the names of Under-Sea. And my wishes were granted. So Lorca of the Island was born."

"But Robert never came to the Island," said Jessie, "because he left the Realm with Princess Jessica that very day. And he couldn't come back."

Lorca bowed her head. "And then—oh, then I began to miss the sea," she cried. "I missed the soft water. I missed my family, my friends. I wanted to be able to swim again, and see the coral and the palaces, and feel the voices of the people I loved."

She drew a deep breath. "I did not like the land. The bright sun hurt my eyes. I hid away from it down here, in this cave. I tried to wish myself back to Under-Sea. I tried with one wish-stone, with ten, with a hundred. But . . ." Her voice trailed away.

"That's why you've been trying to catch the magic fish," sighed Ripple. "Because only he is powerful enough to undo the wish-stone magic."

"Of course!" cried Lorca. "He was my last hope. I wove nets from my hair and threw them into the sea. Those fish I caught I kept, for company. I was so lonely! But the one I really wanted, the magic fish, I never caught. Until this day."

She tore at her long black hair. "And now he says he cannot help me. So I must stay as Lorca forever. And I can never go home again."

Jessie felt her eyes filling with tears.

The magic fish was swimming in small circles of distress. "Coral—Lorca," he bubbled. "I am sorry. But the Rule . . ."

"You don't know for sure!" exclaimed Jessie. "The magic might still work. Try, Lorca. Just try!"

Lorca stared at her, her beautiful face filled with half-fearful hope. She clasped her hands together. She closed her eyes.

"I wish . . ." she began, and swallowed. "I wish—that I—that Lorca of the Island may become Coral of Under-Sea once more."

They waited, holding their breath. The seconds ticked by.

It's not going to happen, thought Jessie. Oh, I can't bear it! She spun round to the magic fish. "You *must* be able to help," she raged. "Forget about the Rule just for once."

The fish looked at her helplessly.

"You were caught and freed," Jessie begged. "Isn't that enough? Oh magic fish, *please* make Lorca's wish come true!"

The fish leaped in the water. "Caught and freed! Yes! Jessie!" he bubbled. "Jessie . . . !"

But before he could say any more there was a low, rumbling, growling sound. Pieces of rock began falling from the ceiling of the cave and splashing into the lake.

"What's happening?" Jessie screamed. "What's gone wrong?"

"The Island! It's sinking!" squeaked the fish.

The rumbling grew louder. The ground on which Jessie and Lorca were standing began to tremble. With a crack the rock split under their feet.

"Dive!" shrieked Ripple.

Jessie snatched Lorca's hand and jumped into the lake. Then they were all swimming for their lives, surrounded by hundreds of other fish that had come streaming in from the sides of the lake.

They raced for the cave that was the entrance to the open sea. Down, down, they swam, as rocks plunged into the lake after them. They darted through the torn net gate, out of the cave entrance.

And then, with seconds to spare, they were plunging into safe water, as Lorca's Island tumbled to the ocean bed behind them.

Jessie spun around to look. Where once the dark shadow had been there was now only cloudy, bubbling water and a pile of rocks and sand. Below the rocks, she knew, the wish-stones lay buried. No one could find them now.

And only then did she remember.

Lorca! she thought, in confusion. Lorca has no coral necklace. She won't be able to breathe. She'll drown.

"No she won't, Jessie!"

"No I won't, Jessie!"

The sweet voices sang in her mind. Soft white hands touched hers. She looked around. She saw Ripple's smile, her floating light brown hair, a flashing silver tail. And beside her, another smile, a cloud of shining black hair, sparkling blue eyes—and another silver tail.

She blinked.

Lorca was gone. Coral was a mermaid again.

A flash of gold beside her caught her eye. It was the magic fish.

"So," she said. "You decided the Rule could be bent after all."

"No," his bubbling voice piped in her ear. "No, Jessie, you don't understand. You—"

"Home!" sang Ripple and Coral, diving and plunging in the blue-green water. "We're going home!"

Home, thought Jessie. Blue Moon. Granny. Mum. *Home*. Her heart ached. She hadn't found what she'd come for in Under-Sea, but suddenly she wanted to be home more than anything in the world. The danger must be very close, now. She was needed there, she had to go. But home seemed so far away.

I wish I was home, right now, she thought, I so wish . . .

The water swirled in front of her eyes. She couldn't see. What's happening? she thought in panic.

"Jessie! Jessie! Where are you? Where . . . ?"

She could hear the mermaids' voices calling, but faintly.

"Goodbye, Jessie," bubbled the magic fish. "I'll tell the others — Ripple, Coral, your friends waiting on the shore. I'll tell them . . . about the wishes . . . your hair . . . goodbye . . . goodbye . . . thank you. . ."

And then his voice too had died away.

ᴛʜe ᴛʜiʀd wiSʜ

Jessie opened her eyes. She blinked in the bright, bright sunlight. She was sitting on the grass in the secret garden. The air smelled of burning leaves and rosemary. Fire-engine sirens howled in the distance.

"Jessie!" Granny was bending over her, stroking her dripping hair. "Oh, Jessie, I've been so worried about you. I should never have let you go. Jessie, we've got to leave here. The fires are coming."

Jessie shook her head, trying to clear it. Drops of salt water sprayed the dry grass. She touched her neck. The coral necklace was gone. "How did

349

I get here?" she murmured. "How . . . ?"

"Don't worry about that now," begged Granny. "Just come."

Jessie stumbled after her as she hurried out of the secret garden, up through the tall trees toward the house. Her mind was racing.

Somehow the magic fish had sent her home. But how? He'd said he couldn't grant wishes just because people asked for them.

But then a few of the things he'd said hadn't been true. He'd said Lorca couldn't make a wish, because she hadn't caught him by accident. And yet her wish to turn back into Coral had been granted.

How strange. He'd been so certain. And it was true that, at first, Jessie had thought he was right. On the Island Lorca had made her wish, but nothing had happened for ages. In fact, nothing had happened till . . .

Jessie stopped. Her jaw dropped. Could it be . . . ?

"Come *on*, Jessie!" shouted Granny from the house.

What had the magic fish called to her as she disappeared from Under-Sea? *"I'll tell them,"* he'd bubbled. *"I'll tell them . . . about the wishes . . . your hair . . ."*

Jessie thought it through. When they had first been caught in Lorca's net, the magic fish had got tangled in her hair. He had been struggling and panicking.

She had been panicking too. But then she'd remembered her mother's words and calmed down. She had soothed Ripple, then she had quietly freed the fish from her hair.

She had *caught* him accidentally. And then she had *freed* him.

She, not Lorca, had been given the three wishes.

Please make Lorca's wish come true! she had cried to the magic fish. That was the first wish, and it had been granted.

I wish I was home, right now she had thought. That was the second wish. And it had been granted too.

Jessie took a breath. She could see Granny running back from the house toward her, calling. The sun beat down overhead. The hot wind blew in her face, bringing with it the smell of smoke.

It was time for the third wish.

"I wish it would rain!" Jessie yelled with all her might. "I wish it would rain and rain until the fires are out!"

There was a shimmer in the air. The whole earth seemed to be holding its breath. And then, where blue sky had been, there was only gray. And the rain was falling. Slowly at first, and then faster and faster. Heavy, steady, cool rain.

Jessie stood in it, hugging Granny, laughing with happiness as the water soaked them both. They watched the rain washing the dry leaves, cooling the hot grass. And they imagined that same rain splashing on hungry flames all over the Mountains, so that they hissed, and grew small, and finally died.

"You found a wish-stone!" Granny breathed.

"No, I didn't," said Jessie.

Granny turned to her in amazement. "Then how —" she began.

"Jessie! Mum!" called a voice. They looked back toward the house. Rosemary was standing there, laughing at them.

"What are you two *doing*?" she shouted.

Jessie grinned. "Getting wet! Again!" she called. She ran through the tall trees, up the steps that led to Blue Moon, and into her mother's arms.

Rosemary hugged her tightly. She didn't seem to care that Jessie was dripping wet.

"Oh, Jessie, the rain!" she sighed. "Oh, isn't it wonderful? And it was so sudden. Like magic."

Jessie snuggled against her. "Magic is useful," she said. "But human common sense helps a lot too."

Rosemary stroked her daughter's tangled, wet hair. That was a strange thing to say, she thought. But she decided not to ask any questions. It had been a long, hot day, and Jessie was probably over-tired. It was a shame she hadn't been able to have a swim.

Two days later, Jessie woke to find that the rain had stopped in the night. The morning sun was beaming through her window. The curtains fluttered in a light breeze. Everything outside looked fresh and new.

She saw something lying on her desk. She got out of bed and went to look. It was the sundress she had left on the shore of the Bay. It was clean, ironed and folded, and smelled of flowers.

"Thank you, Patrice," she whispered. She picked up the dress and took it to her cupboard. As she hung it up she felt something in the pocket—something small and hard, wrapped in a scrap of silk.

She pulled it out and unwrapped it. It was a tiny golden fish. Another charm for her bracelet. Another gift from the Realm, so she'd never forget.

Jessie held the little fish to her cheek for a moment. The memories of Under-Sea came flooding back.

She shivered as she remembered Lorca's Island. She smiled as she thought of Ripple and Coral, Aqua and Storm, the crystal palaces, the coral gardens, the tiny water-fairies on their seahorses, the ride down the river. She laughed aloud at the memory of the magic fish.

"You sound happy," said her mother at the door.

Jessie turned around. "I am," she said. "I'm so, so happy."

"It's going to be a lovely day," Rosemary went on. "And I'm not working this morning. Would you like to go to the pool? It's been ages since you had a swim."

Jessie laughed again. "I'd *love* a swim," she said. "In fact, I can't think of anything I'd rather do."

"You see? Wishes *can* come true," teased Rosemary.

Jessie looked at the little golden fish in her hand and at the other charms on her bracelet.

"Yes," she said. "I know."

EMILY RODDA

has written many books for children, including the Deltora Quest and Rowan of Rin books. She has won the Children's Book Council of Australia Book of the Year Award a unprecented five times, and her books have been translated into twenty-four languages and published in thirty countries. A former editor, Ms. Rodda has also written adult mysteries under the name Jennifer Rowe. She lives in Australia. You can visit her online at www.emilyrodda.com.

For exclusive information on your favorite authors and artists, visit www.authortracker.com.